UNWIN HYMAN

CW00728397

FREE

AS I

KNOW

INCLUDING
FOLLOW ON
ACTIVITIES

EDITED BY BEVERLEY NAIDOO

Published by
UNWIN HYMAN LIMITED
15/17 Broadwick Street
London W1V 1FP

Selection and notes © Beverley Naidoo 1987
The copyright of each story and poem remains the property of the
author

First published in 1987 by Bell & Hyman
Reprinted by Unwin Hyman Limited 1990

Free as I know. – (Unwin Hyman collections)
    1. English literature
    I. Naidoo, Beverley
    820.8   PR1109

ISBN 0–7135–2807–9

Printed in Great Britain by
Billing & Sons Ltd., Worcester

Series cover design by Iain Lanyon
Cover illustration by Eric Velasquez

CONTENTS   *Page*

Introduction

Each of us can probably point to some particular experiences in childhood or adolescence which we feel have played an important part in shaping our perceptions, perhaps even personality. The idea of seminal experiences–those which contain the seeds of change and which are capable of influencing us–is central to this collection. Indeed they are the stuff of literature and my first criterion in selecting these extracts from novels and autobiographies, short stories and poems was that they should reflect in some way young people gaining insights into their various societies, as well as contending with powerful forces within them.

My own fascination with experiences which change people owes a great deal to the fact that I underwent a profound change of attitudes myself around the age of eighteen. It was the year in which I became conscious of the artificially-constructed blinkers of racist prejudice which were distorting my vision as a white South African. As I began the struggle to remove them, for the first time I began to see the society around me in its full dimension. It was a shock. I had been brought up accepting the usual misrepresentations of reality and false justifications with which most white people cloaked the real nature of their behaviour towards those whom they denied justice.

My education thus began at a rather late age, outside the class-room...education in the real sense of being led out of my own narrow perceptions and having to respond to a whole range of human experiences which for eighteen years I had either ignored, or learnt to misinterpret. Much of what I saw was deeply painful and was a direct result of the system which gave me and my white community its privileges. Yet we could still deceive ourselves that we were 'moral' human beings, upholders of 'civilised' values!

It is, of course, not only in the white South African community that young people can grow up with a narrow, blinkered view of their society and their own role within it. Any group which has advantage over another is unlikely to encourage questioning of the relationship. All over the world people who are disadvantaged have difficulty in making their voices heard. For every book in which one can hear such voices, there are hundreds of others in which they are completely absent.

From this followed a second criterion in selecting texts for this collection...that the perspectives revealed would be those which are often passed over. I particularly looked for pieces which were challenging and which would encourage readers to clarify their own responses, whatever they may be.

6

Literature has the tremendous quality of allowing us to engage imaginatively in the lives of others. It enables us to move beyond ourselves and our own experiences. If we allow ourselves to respond to it fully, it can be a great educator. For those of us brought up monoculturally, literature which springs from outside our own boundaries can be a life-line. A third and equally important criterion has therefore been that the collection contain stimulating literature of an international character.

The pieces are arranged in a broadly chronological order. The extracts from *Tell Freedom* and *I Know Why The Caged Bird Sings* depict powerful autobiographical experiences of the authors in the 1920s and '30s in South Africa and the USA respectively. Although they span the Atlantic, the connections are vivid.

Basketball Game and 'Private Eloy' are set in the 1950s in the United States and Cuba respectively. Each of the central characters is faced with a difficult choice–to go with the system or against it–and they choose differently. For one of them the consequences are fatal. I hope readers will be unable to resist considering 'What if I....?'

I imagine 'Small Avalanches' taking place around the '50s too, although the nature of the experience (a potential threat to a teenage girl) and the nature of the setting (the hot, dusty, sparse landscape of Colorado) gives the story an all too timeless quality.

Hand On The Sun and 'Young Gifted And Black' both derive from experiences in England in the 1960s and 1970. The former reveals emotion close to despair, which instead turned to anger in a new generation of young black people determined not to accept the same terms of submission as their parents. The latter portrays my own sense of the mood of regeneration and spirited youthful resistance emerging at the time.

'India' and 'True Grit, Hard Graft' are also English in origin but the voices are from the 1980s. They contain an independent confidence, bearing out Maya Angelou's words: 'But still, like dust, I'll rise'.

'Homecoming' and 'If Someone Were To Ask Me...' are responses to the continuing, living horrors of apartheid in the 1980s, written by two young people who both have family roots in South Africa.

With *Brother In The Land* readers are moved to an indeterminate point in the future...such as might be in post-nuclear Britain. What qualities would be required by any survivors in a 'landscape of poisonous desolation'?

The collection ends with two poems by young writers who have contrasting views. Are children simple innocents who cannot avoid contamination as they grow up into an ugly adult world, or are they capable of an inner strength to be as 'free as I know'?

I hope this collection will arouse readers to respond strongly, with both heart and mind. The Follow On activities for discussion and writing have been devised to meet GCSE requirements for students studying English and English Literature, providing a wide variety of suggestions for coursework and ideas for written and oral responses, including extended studies. Teachers are recommended to preview the relevant Follow On section in advance of reading each text with students.

BEVERLEY NAIDOO

PETER ABRAHAMS

$\mathcal{A}$n extract from
'Tell Freedom'

*When Peter Abrahams was five his father died and the
family lost their home in town. This was South Africa in
the 1920s–long before the word 'apartheid' had been
coined. But not to be white has always meant trouble.
The five-year old boy–called Lee here–found himself
separated from mother, brother and sisters and taken to
unknown relatives in a remote country area.*

Wednesday was crackling day. On that day the children of the
location made the long trek to Elsberg siding for the squares of
pig's rind that passed for our daily meat. We collected a double
lot of cow dung the day before; a double lot of *moeroga*[1].

I finished my breakfast and washed up. Aunt Liza was at her
wash-tub in the yard. A misty, sickly sun was just showing.
And on the open veld the frost lay thick and white on the
grass.

'Ready?' Aunt Liza called.

I went out to her. She shook the soapsuds off her swollen
hands and wiped them on her apron. She lifted the apron and
put her hand through the slits of the many thin cotton dresses
she wore. The dress nearest the skin was the one with the
pocket. From this she pulled a sixpenny piece. She tied it in a
knot in the corner of a bit of coloured cloth.

'Take care of that... Take the smaller piece of bread in the bin
but don't eat it till you start back. You can have a small piece of
crackling with it. Only a small piece, understand?'

'Yes, Aunt Liza.'

'All right.'

I got the bread and tucked it into the little canvas bag in

9

which I would carry the crackling.

'Bye Aunt Liza.' I trotted off, one hand in my pocket, feeling the cloth where the money was. I paused at Andries's home.

'Andries!' I danced up and down while I waited. The cold was not so terrible on bare feet if one did not keep still.

Andries came trotting out of their yard. His mother's voice followed; desperate and plaintive:

'I'll skin you if you lose the money!'

'Women!' Andries said bitterly.

I glimpsed the dark, skinny woman at her wash-tub as we trotted across the veld. Behind, and in front of us, other children trotted in twos and threes.

There was a sharp bite to the morning air I sucked in; it stung my nose so that tears came to my eyes; it went down my throat like an icy draught; my nose ran. I tried breathing through my mouth but this was worse. The cold went through my shirt and shorts; my skin went pimply and chilled; my fingers went numb and began to ache; my feet felt like frozen lumps that did not belong to me, yet jarred and hurt each time I put them down. I began to feel sick and desperate.

'Jesus God in heaven!' Andries cried suddenly.

I looked at him. His eyes were rimmed in red. Tears ran down his cheeks. His face was drawn and purple, a sick look on it.

'Faster,' I said.

'Think it'll help?'

I nodded. We went faster. We passed two children, sobbing and moaning as they ran. We were all in the same desperate situation. We were creatures haunted and hounded by the cold. It was a cruel enemy who gave no quarter. And our means of fighting it were pitifully inadequate. In all the mornings and evenings of the winter months, young and old, big and small, were helpless victims of the bitter cold. Only towards noon and the early afternoon, when the sun sat high in the sky, was there a brief respite. For us, the children, the cold, especially the morning cold, assumed an awful and malevolent personality. We talked of 'It'. 'It' was a half-human monster with evil thoughts, evil intentions, bent on destroying us. 'It' was happiest when we were most miserable.

Andries had told me how 'It' had, last winter, caught and killed a boy.

Hunger was an enemy too, but one with whom we could come to terms, who had many virtues and values. Hunger gave our *pap*[2], *moeroga*, and crackling, a feast-like quality. We could, when it was not with us, think and talk kindly about it. Its memory could even give moments of laughter. But the cold of winter was with us all the time. 'It' never really eased up. There were only more bearable degrees of 'It' at high noon and on mild days. 'It' was the real enemy. And on this Wednesday morning, as we ran across the veld, winter was more bitterly, bitingly, freezingly, real than ever.

The sun climbed. The frozen earth thawed, leaving the short grass looking wet and weary. Painfully, our feet and legs came alive. The aching numbness slowly left our fingers. We ran more slowly in the more bearable cold.

In climbing, the sun lost some of its damp look and seemed a real, if cold, sun. When it was right overhead, we struck the sandy road which meant we were nearing the siding. None of the others were in sight. Andries and I were alone on the sandy road on the open veld. We slowed down to a brisk walk. We were sufficiently thawed to want to talk.

'How far?' I said.

'A few minutes,' he said.

'I've got a piece of bread,' I said.

'Me too,' he said. 'Let's eat it now.'

'On the way back,' I said. 'With a bit of crackling.'

'Good idea... Race to the fork.'

'All right.'

'Go!' he said.

We shot off together, legs working like pistons. He soon pulled away from me. He reached the fork in the road some fifty yards ahead.

'I win!' he shouted gleefully, though his teeth still chattered.

We pitched stones down the road, each trying to pitch further than the other. I won and wanted to go on doing it. But Andries soon grew weary with pitching. We raced again. Again he won. He wanted another race but I refused. I wanted pitching, but he refused. So, sulking with each other, we reached the pig farm.

We followed a fenced-off pathway round sprawling white buildings. Everywhere about us was the grunt of pigs. As we passed an open doorway, a huge dog came bounding out, snarling and barking at us. In our terror, we forgot it was fenced in and streaked away. Surprised, I found myself a good distance ahead of Andries. We looked back and saw a young white woman call the dog to heel.

'Damn Boer dog,' Andries said.

'Matter with it?' I asked.

'They teach them to go for us. Never get caught by one. My old man's got a hole in his bottom where a Boer dog got him.'

I remembered I had outstripped him.

'I won!' I said.

'Only because you were frightened,' he said.

'I still won.'

'Scare arse,' he jeered.

'Scare arse, yourself!'

'I'll knock you!'

'I'll knock you back!'

A couple of white men came down the path and ended our possible fight. We hurried past them to the distant shed where a queue had already formed. There were grown-ups and children. All the grown-ups, and some of the children, were from places other than our location.

The line moved slowly. The young white man who served us did it in leisurely fashion, with long pauses for a smoke. Occasionally he turned his back.

At last, after what seemed hours, my turn came. Andries was behind me. I took the sixpenny piece from the square of cloth and offered it to the man.

'Well?' he said.

'Sixpence crackling, please.'

Andries nudged me in the back. The man's stare suddenly became cold and hard. Andries whispered in my ear.

'Well?' the man repeated coldly.

'Please *baas*,' I said.

'What d'you want?'

'Sixpence crackling, please.'

'What?'

Andries dug me in the ribs.

'Sixpence crackling, please *baas.*'

'What?'

'Sixpence crackling, please *baas.*'

'You new here?'

'Yes, *baas.*' I looked at his feet while he stared at me.

At last he took the sixpenny piece from me. I held my bag open while he filled it with crackling from a huge pile on a large canvas sheet on the ground. Turning away, I stole a fleeting glance at his face. His eyes met mine, and there was amused, challenging mockery in them. I waited for Andries at the back of the queue, out of the reach of the white man's mocking eyes.

The cold day was at its mildest as we walked home along the sandy road. I took out my piece of bread and, with a small piece of greasy crackling, still warm, on it, I munched as we went along. We had not yet made our peace so Andries munched his bread and crackling on the other side of the road.

'Dumb fool!' he mocked at me for not knowing how to address the white man.

'Scare arse!' I shouted back.

Thus, hurling curses at each other, we reached the fork. Andries saw them first and moved over to my side of the road.

'White boys,' he said.

There were three of them. Two of about our own size and one slightly bigger. They had school bags and were coming towards us up the road from the siding.

'Better run for it,' Andries said.

'Why?'

'No, that'll draw them. Let's just walk along, but quickly.'

'Why?' I repeated.

'Shut up,' he said.

Some of his anxiety touched me. Our own scrape was forgotten. We marched side by side as fast as we could. The white boys saw us and hurried up the road. We passed the fork. Perhaps they would take the turning away from us. We dared not look back.

'Hear them?' Andries asked.

'No.'

I looked over my shouder.

'They're coming,' I said.

'Walk faster,' Andries said. 'If they come closer, run.'

'Hey, *klipkop*[3]!'

'Don't look back,' Andries said.

'Hottentot!'

We walked as fast as we could.

'Bloody kaffir!'

Ahead was a bend in the road. Behind the bend were bushes. Once there, we could run without them knowing it till it was too late.

'Faster,' Andries said.

They began pelting us with stones.

'Run when we get to the bushes,' Andries said.

The bend and the bushes were near. We would soon be there.

A clear young voice carried to us:

'Your fathers are dirty black bastards of baboons!'

'Run!' Andries called.

A violent, unreasoning anger suddenly possessed me. I stopped and turned.

'You're a liar!' I screamed it.

The foremost boy pointed at me:

'An ugly black baboon!'

In a fog of rage I went towards him.

'Liar!' I shouted. 'My father was better than your father!'

I neared them. The bigger boy stepped between me and the one I was after.

'My father was better than your father! Liar!'

The big boy struck me a mighty clout on the side of the face. I staggered, righted myself, and leapt at the boy who had insulted my father. I struck him on the face, hard. A heavy blow on the back of my head nearly stunned me. I grabbed at the boy in front of me. We went down together.

'Liar!' I said through clenched teeth, hitting him with all my might.

Blows rained on me, on my head, my neck, the side of my face, my mouth, but my enemy was under me and I pounded him fiercely, all the time repeating:

'Liar! Liar! Liar!'

Suddenly, stars exploded in my head. Then there was darkness.

I emerged from the darkness to find Andries kneeling beside me.

'God man! I thought they'd killed you.'

I sat up. The white boys were nowhere to be seen. Like Andries, they'd probably thought me dead and run off in panic. The inside of my mouth felt sore and swollen. My nose was tender to the touch. The back of my head ached. A trickle of blood dripped from my nose. I stemmed it with the square of coloured cloth. The greatest damage was to my shirt. It was ripped in many places. I remembered the crackling. I looked anxiously about. It was safe, a little off the road on the grass. I relaxed. I got up and brushed my clothes. I picked up the crackling.

'God, you're dumb!' Andries said. 'You're going to get it! Dumb arse!'

I was too depressed to retort. Besides, I knew he was right. I was dumb. I should have run when he told me to.

'Come on,' I said.

One of many small groups of children, each child carrying his little bag of crackling, we trod the long road home in the cold winter afternoon.

There was tension in the house that night. When I got back Aunt Liza had listened to the story in silence. The beating or scolding I expected did not come. But Aunt Liza changed while she listened, became remote and withdrawn. When Uncle Sam came home she told him what had happened. He, too, just looked at me and became more remote and withdrawn than usual. They were waiting for something; their tension reached out to me, and I waited with them, anxious, apprehensive.

The thing we waited for came while we were having our supper. We heard a trap pull up outside.

'Here it is,' Uncle Sam said and got up.

Aunt Liza leaned back from the table and put her hands in

her lap, fingers intertwined, a cold, unseeing look in her eyes.

Before Uncle Sam reached it, the door burst open. A tall, broad, white man strode in. Behind him came the three boys. The one I had attacked had swollen lips and a puffy left eye.

'Evening *baas*,' Uncle Sam murmured.

'That's him,' the bigger boy said, pointing at me.

The white man stared till I lowered my eyes.

'Well?' he said.

'He's sorry, *baas*,' Uncle Sam said quickly. 'I've given him a hiding he won't forget soon. You know how it is, *baas*. He's new here, the child of a relative in Johannesburg and they don't all know how to behave there. You know how it is in the big towns, *baas*.' The plea in Uncle Sam's voice had grown more pronounced as he went on. He turned to me. 'Tell the *baas* and young *basies* how sorry you are, Lee.'

I looked at Aunt Liza and something in her lifelessness made me stubborn in spite of my fear.

'He insulted my father,' I said.

The white man smiled.

'See Sam, your hiding couldn't have been good.'

There was a flicker of life in Aunt Liza's eyes. For a brief moment she saw me, looked at me, warmly, lovingly, then her eyes went dead again.

'He's only a child, *baas*,' Uncle Sam murmured.

'You stubborn too, Sam?'

'No, *baas*.'

'Good… Then teach him, Sam. If you and he are to live here, you must teach him. Well…?'

'Yes, *baas*.'

Uncle Sam went into the other room and returned with a thick leather thong. He wound it once round his hand and advanced on me. The man and boys leaned against the door, watching. I looked at Aunt Liza's face. Though there was no sign of life or feeling on it, I knew suddenly, instinctively, that she wanted me not to cry.

Bitterly, Uncle Sam said:

'You must never lift your hand to a white person. No matter what happens, you must never lift your hand to a white person…'

16

He lifted the strap and brought it down on my back. I clenched my teeth and stared at Aunt Liza. I did not cry with the first three strokes. Then, suddenly, Aunt Liza went limp. Tears showed in her eyes. The thong came down on my back, again and again. I screamed and begged for mercy. I grovelled at Uncle Sam's feet, begging him to stop, promising never to lift my hand to any white person...

At last, the white man's voice said:

'All right, Sam.'

Uncle Sam stopped. I lay whimpering on the floor. Aunt Liza sat like one in a trance.

'Is he still stubborn, Sam?'

'Tell the *baas* and *basies* you are sorry.'

'I'm sorry,' I said.

'Bet his father is one of those who believe in equality.'

'His father is dead,' Aunt Liza said.

'Good night, Sam.'

'Good night, *baas*. Sorry about this.'

'All right, Sam.' He opened the door. The boys went out first, then he followed. 'Good night, Liza.'

Aunt Liza did not answer. The door shut behind the white folk, and, soon, we heard their trap moving away. Uncle Sam flung the thong viciously against the door, slumped down on the bench, folded his arms on the table, and buried his head on his arms. Aunt Liza moved away from him, came on the floor beside me and lifted me into her large lap. She sat rocking my body. Uncle Sam began to sob softly. After some time, he raised his head and looked at us.

'Explain to the child, Liza,' he said.

'You explain,' Aunt Liza said bitterly. 'You are the man. You did the beating. You are the head of the family. This is a man's world. You do the explaining.'

'Please, Liza...'

'You should be happy. The whites are satisfied. We can go on now.'

With me in her arms, Aunt Liza got up. She carried me into the other room. The food on the table remained half-eaten. She laid me on the bed on my stomach, smeared fat on my back, then covered me with the blankets. She undressed and got into bed beside me. She cuddled me close, warmed me with her own body. With her big hand on my cheek, she rocked me, first to silence, then to sleep.

For the only time of my stay there, I slept on a bed in Elsberg.

When I woke next morning Uncle Sam had gone. Aunt Liza only once referred to the beating he had given me. It was in the late afternoon, when I returned with the day's cow dung.

'It hurt him,' she said. 'You'll understand one day.'

That night, Uncle Sam brought me an orange, a bag of boiled sweets, and a dirty old picture book. He smiled as he gave them to me, rather anxiously. When I smiled back at him, he seemed to relax. He put his hand on my head, started to say something, then changed his mind and took his seat by the fire.

Aunt Liza looked up from the floor where she dished out the food.

'It's all right, old man,' she murmured.

'One day...' Uncle Sam said.

'It's all right,' Aunt Liza repeated insistently.

1 *wild spinach*
2 *porridge made from corn-meal*
3 *an insult*

*a*n extract from
'*I Know Why The Caged Bird Sings*'

Maya Angelou's real name was Marguerite. She acquired the name 'Maya' through her brother Bailey who was one year older and who insisted in his early years on calling her 'Mya Sister'. This extract comes from her first book of autobiography and the year is 1938, in the southern state of Arkansas, USA.

Recently a white woman from Texas, who would quickly describe herself as a liberal, asked me about my hometown. When I told her that in Stamps my grandmother had owned the only Negro general merchandise store since the turn of the century, she exclaimed, 'Why, you were a debutante.' Ridiculous and even ludicrous. But Negro girls in small Southern towns, whether poverty-stricken or just munching along on a few of life's necessities, were given as extensive and irrelevant preparations for adulthood as rich white girls shown in magazines. Admittedly the training was not the same. While white girls learned to waltz and sit gracefully with a tea cup balanced on their knees, we were lagging behind, learning the mid-Victorian values with very little money to indulge them.

We were required to embroider and I had trunkfuls of colorful dishtowels, pillowcases, runners and handkerchiefs to my credit. I mastered the art of crocheting and tatting, and there was a lifetime's supply of dainty doilies that would never be used in sacheted dresser drawers. It went without saying that all girls could iron and wash, but the finer touches around the home, like setting a table with real silver, baking roasts and cooking vegetables without meat, had to be learned elsewhere. Usually at the source of those habits. During my tenth year, a white woman's kitchen became my finishing school.

Mrs. Viola Cullinan was a plump woman who lived in a three-bedroom house somewhere behind the post office. She was singularly unattractive until she smiled, and then the lines around her eyes and mouth which made her look perpetually dirty disappeared, and her face looked like the mask of an impish elf. She usually rested her smile until late afternoon when her women friends dropped in and Miss Glory, the cook, served them cold drinks on the closed-in porch.

The exactness of her house was inhuman. This glass went here and only here. That cup had its place and it was an act of impudent rebellion to place it anywhere else. At twelve o'clock the table was set. At 12:15 Mrs. Cullinan sat down to dinner (whether her husband had arrived or not). At 12:16 Miss Glory brought out the food.

It took me a week to learn the difference between a salad plate, a bread plate and a dessert plate.

Mrs. Cullinan kept up the tradition of her wealthy parents. She was from Virginia. Miss Glory, who was a descendant of slaves that had worked for the Cullinans, told me her history. She had married beneath her (according to Miss Glory). Her husband's family hadn't had their money very long and what they had 'didn't 'mount to much.'

As ugly as she was, I thought privately, she was lucky to get a husband above or beneath her station. But Miss Glory wouldn't let me say a thing against her mistress. She was very patient with me, however, over the housework. She explained the dishware, silverware and servants' bells. The large round bowl in which soup was served wasn't a soup bowl, it was a tureen. There were goblets, sherbet glasses, ice-cream glasses, wine glasses, green glass coffee cups with matching saucers, and water glasses. I had a glass to drink from, and it sat with Miss Glory's on a separate shelf from the others. Soup spoons, gravy boat, butter knives, salad forks and carving platter were additions to my vocabulary and in fact almost represented a new language. I was fascinated with the novelty, with the fluttering Mrs. Cullinan and her Alice-in-Wonder-land house.

Her husband remains, in my memory, undefined. I lumped him with all the other white men that I had ever seen and tried not to see.

On our way home one evening, Miss Glory told me that Mrs. Cullinan couldn't have children. She said that she was too delicate-boned. It was hard to imagine bones at all under those layers of fat. Miss Glory went on to say that the doctor had taken out all her lady organs. I reasoned that a pig's organs included the lungs, heart and liver, so if Mrs. Cullinan was walking around without those essentials, it explained why she drank alcohol out of unmarked bottles. She was keeping herself embalmed.

When I spoke to Bailey about it, he agreed that I was right, but he also informed me that Mr. Cullinan had two daughters by a colored lady and that I knew them very well. He added that the girls were the spitting image of their father. I was unable to remember what he looked like, although I had just left him a few hours before, but I thought of the Coleman girls. They were very light-skinned and certainly didn't look very much like their mother (no one ever mentioned Mr. Coleman).

My pity for Mrs. Cullinan preceded me the next morning like the Cheshire cat's smile. Those girls, who could have been her daughters, were beautiful. They didn't have to straighten their hair. Even when they were caught in the rain, their braids still hung down straight like tamed snakes. Their mouths were pouty little cupid's bows. Mrs. Cullinan didn't know what she missed. Or maybe she did. Poor Mrs. Cullinan.

For weeks after, I arrived early, left late and tried very hard to make up for her barrenness. If she had had her own children, she wouldn't have had to ask me to run a thousand errands from her back door to the back door of her friends. Poor old Mrs. Cullinan.

Then one evening Miss Glory told me to serve the ladies on the porch. After I set the tray down and turned toward the kitchen, one of the women asked, 'What's your name, girl?' It was the speckled-faced one. Mrs Cullinan said, 'She doesn't talk much. Her name's Margaret.'

'Is she dumb?'

'No. As I understand it, she can talk when she wants to but she's usually quiet as a little mouse. Aren't you, Margaret?'

I smiled at her. Poor thing. No organs and couldn't even pronounce my name correctly.

'She's a sweet little thing, though.'

'Well, that may be, but the name's too long. I'd never bother myself. I'd call her Mary if I was you.'

I fumed into the kitchen. That horrible woman would never have the chance to call me Mary because if I was starving I'd never work for her. I decided I wouldn't pee on her if her heart was on fire. Giggles drifted in off the porch and into Miss Glory's pots. I wondered what they could be laughing about.

That evening I decided to write a poem on being white, fat, old and without children. It was going to be a tragic ballad. I would have to watch her carefully to capture the essence of her loneliness and pain.

The very next day, she called me by the wrong name. Miss Glory and I were washing up the lunch dishes when Mrs. Cullinan came to the doorway. 'Mary?'

Miss Glory asked, 'Who?'

Mrs. Cullinan, sagging a little, knew and I knew. 'I want Mary to go down to Mrs. Randall's and take her some soup. She's not been feeling well for a few days.'

Miss Glory's face was a wonder to see. 'You mean Margaret, ma'am. Her name's Margaret.'

'That's too long. She's Mary from now on. Heat that soup from last night and put it in the china tureen and, Mary, I want you to carry it carefully.'

Every person I knew had a hellish horror of being 'called out of his name.' It was a dangerous practice to call a Negro anything that could be loosely construed as insulting because of the centuries of their having been called niggers, jigs, dinges, blackbirds, crows, boots and spooks.

Miss Glory had a fleeting second of feeling sorry for me. Then as she handed me the hot tureen she said, 'Don't mind, don't pay that no mind. Sticks and stones may break your bones, but words . . . You know, I been working for her for twenty years.'

She held the back door open for me. 'Twenty years. I wasn't much older than you. My name used to be Hallelujah. That's what Ma named me, but my mistress give me 'Glory,' and it stuck. I likes it better too.'

I was in the little path that ran behind the houses when Miss Glory shouted, 'It's shorter too.'

For a few seconds it was a tossup over whether I would laugh (imagine being named Hallelujah) or cry (imagine letting some white woman rename you for her convenience). My anger saved me from either outburst. I had to quit the job, but the problem was going to be how to do it. Momma wouldn't allow me to quit for just any reason.

'She's a peach. That woman is a real peach.' Mrs. Randall's maid was talking as she took the soup from me, and I wondered what her name used to be and what she answered to now.

For a week I looked into Mrs. Cullinan's face as she called me Mary. She ignored my coming late and leaving early. Miss Glory was a little annoyed because I had begun to leave egg yolk on the dishes and wasn't putting much heart in polishing the silver. I hoped that she would complain to our boss, but she didn't.

Then Bailey solved my dilemma. He had me describe the contents of the cupboard and the particular plates she liked best. Her favorite piece was a casserole shaped like a fish and the green glass coffee cups. I kept his instructions in mind, so on the next day when Miss Glory was hanging out clothes and I had again been told to serve the old biddies on the porch, I dropped the empty serving tray. When I heard Mrs. Cullinan scream, 'Mary!' I picked up the casserole and two of the green glass cups in readiness. As she rounded the kitchen door I let them fall on the tiled floor.

I could never absolutely describe to Bailey what happened next, because each time I got to the part where she fell on the floor and screwed up her ugly face to cry, we burst out laughing. She actually wobbled around on the floor and picked up shards of the cups and cried, 'Oh, Momma. Oh, dear Gawd. It's Momma's china from Virginia. Oh, Momma, I sorry.'

Miss Glory came running in from the yard and the women

from the porch crowded around. Miss Glory was almost as broken up as her mistress. 'You mean to say she broke our Virginia dishes? What we gone do?'

Mrs. Cullinan cried louder, 'That clumsy nigger. Clumsy little black nigger.'

Old speckled-face leaned down and asked, 'Who did it, Viola? Was it Mary? Who did it?'

Everything was happening so fast I can't remember whether her action preceded her words, but I know that Mrs. Cullinan said, 'Her name's Margaret, goddamn it, her name's Margaret.' And she threw a wedge of the broken plate at me. It could have been the hysteria which put her aim off, but the flying crockery caught Miss Glory right over her ear and she started screaming.

I left the front door wide open so all the neighbors could hear.

Mrs. Cullinan was right about one thing. My name wasn't Mary.

Still I Rise

You may write me down in history
With your bitter, twisted lies,
You may trod me in the very dirt
But still, like dust, I'll rise.

Does my sassiness upset you?
Why are you beset with gloom?
'Cause I walk like I've got oil wells
Pumping in my living room.

Just like moons and like suns,
With the certainty of tides,
Just like hopes springing high,
Still I'll rise.

Did you want to see me broken?
Bowed head and lowered eyes?
Shoulders falling down like teardrops,
Weakened by my soulful cries.

Does my haughtiness offend you?
Don't you take it awful hard
'Cause I laugh like I've got gold mines
Diggin' in my own back yard.

You may shoot me with your words,
You may cut me with your eyes,
You may kill me with your hatefulness,
But still, like air, I'll rise.

Does my sexiness upset you?
Does it come as a surprise
That I dance like I've got diamonds
At the meeting of my thighs?

Out of the huts of history's shame
I rise

25

Up from a past that's rooted in pain
I rise
I'm a black ocean, leaping and wide,
Welling and swelling I bear in the tide.

Leaving behind nights of terror and fear
I rise
Into a daybreak that's wondrously clear
I rise
Bringing the gifts that my ancestors gave,
I am the dream and the hope of the slave.
I rise
I rise
I rise.

Maya Angelou

*a*n extract from 'Basketball Game'

It is 1956 and Allen's family are the first black people to move into a white neighbourhood of a southern city in the United States. Soon all the other houses have 'For Sale' notices outside. Allen's father tries to warn him off associating with the white girl next door, but she seems determined to be friendly.

Every Saturday Allen's parents went shopping. Allen usually went too, but this Saturday he decided to stay home. They hadn't been gone long when he went out to the driveway, the basketball under his arm. As he played he was very conscious of every basket he made. He practised shooting with his left hand and made more than he missed. He wanted to be good with either hand. Although he never looked toward her house, he presumed she was watching. At least she knew he was there. The sound of the ball hitting the backboard and bounding on the driveway couldn't be ignored, and it wasn't long before he heard a door slam.

He looked around and saw her running across the back-yard.

'Hi, Allen!'

'Hi!' he returned, smiling shyly. He looked at her teeth and was surprised to see the metal gone. And for the first time he thought she was pretty. Not as pretty as Ingrid or Gloria, but pretty nonetheless. Her brown hair was cut short and hung down around her ears. Her face was round and she had thin lips. But what fascinated him most were her eyes. He'd noticed them before and sometimes he thought they were

27

brown, but other times they appeared to be green. This morning they looked yellow. He wished that he had eyes that changed colors. His eyes were so dark that one didn't know if they were brown or black. He wasn't sure himself.

'Can I play some ball with you?'

'Sure.'

She climbed over the low fence. 'You're going to beat me, I know. You're so good.'

'I'm not that good. And it's easy when there's nobody playing but you.' He sounded more at ease with her than he really was. He wanted to turn around to see if anyone was looking but stopped himself. If you pretended everything was normal, well, maybe it would be. He threw the ball to her and she bounced it clumsily a couple of times and shot it toward the basket. It hit the rim and bounced away. Allen chased it up the driveway and threw it back to her. 'Take another one.' She bounced the ball and shot again, awkwardly thrusting her arms out and releasing the ball. It bounced off the rim and onto the lawn, hitting the clothesline pole. Allen picked the ball up, dribbled back on the driveway, spun around, jumped, and shot. The ball bounced off the backboard, hit the front of the rim, and richocheted off.

'Seems like I brought you bad luck.'

'Oh, I miss more often than you think,' he conceded.

They took turns shooting for a while and eventually Rebecca made a basket. 'You want to play a game?' she asked.

He looked surprised. 'Sure.'

'I know you're going to beat me.'

'Don't be too sure,' he said, knowing that he was going to beat her. 'You take it out of bounds first.' He pointed up the driveway to a drainpipe hanging down the side of the house. 'That's out. The fence is out and the grass is out. OK?'

'OK.'

Rebecca bounced the ball clumsily down the driveway. Several times she double dribbled but Allen didn't say anything. It didn't make any difference since he knew he could beat her. She slowly made her way toward the basket, Allen waving his hands in front of her face. He could have easily stolen the ball from her but didn't. She stopped dribbling, grabbed the ball, and drove toward the basket. Instead of jumping with her to block the shot, Allen moved back and she scored.

'You just let me do that,' she told him.

He didn't say anything, not sure why he'd let her do it. He took the ball up the driveway and began dribbling back toward the basket. Rebecca guarded him closely, slapping at the ball several times and missing, but hitting his arm. He maintained control of the ball, and as he leapt to shoot she pushed him, knocking him down. His shot didn't go in.

'Hey, that's a foul,' he said, getting up slowly.

'Oh, we ain't playing by the rules are we? You know you're lots better than I am. I have to do something to try and even things up, don't I? And anyway, you're a boy.'

That was true, he thought, so he brushed himself off as Rebecca took the ball out of bounds. But each time she went in for a lay-up, which was the only shot she knew, Allen found himself moving aside and letting her make it. And every time he had the ball, she pushed him, bumped him, and did anything she could to distract him. He wanted to do the same thing to her, but for some reason he couldn't.

'I won!' she shouted happily. 'I beat you! Let's play another game.'

He shook his head. 'Uh-uh. I don't want to get beat twice in one day.'

'Chicken!' she teased, pushing him playfully. Just then they heard what they thought was a car pulling into her driveway. It was on the other side of her house and they couldn't see it. 'Gotta go, Allen. Maybe I'll see you later.' And before he could reply, she was leaping over the low fence and running across her yard. Just before she went into her house she waved to him. He waved back and had just lowered his hand when he saw her father's car come into view and stop in front of their garage. Allen pretended to be examining his basketball as Rebecca's parents got out of their car.

He wondered if her father had said something to her about him. The way she'd jumped over the fence and run in the house when they heard the car made him think that her father didn't want her talking to him any more than his father wanted him talking to her. Yet she'd come over that morning anyway. She acted like she didn't care what her father thought. And as long as she acted that way, Allen knew he couldn't act any differently. She wasn't afraid of him, so why should he be afraid of her?

Every day he played basketball now and sometimes he saw her getting in the car with her parents or going to empty the trash, but she didn't wave to him. That proved that her parents didn't want her to be his friend. But one morning he saw her parents get in their car and back out of the driveway, and he was sure that they hadn't even gotten to the corner before the back door slammed and there she was, running across the yard, her hair flopping up and down around her face. It was OK, because his father had already gone to his office at the church where he spent most of each day. His mother was home, though, but he didn't think she would say anything. She didn't seem to be afraid of white people.

'Hi, Allen!'

'Hi, Rebecca!'

'Boy, I thought they'd never go somewhere.'

He tightened when he heard her say 'boy' but decided that she hadn't meant anything.

'My father doesn't want me to play with you,' she continued matter-of-factly.

Allen didn't say anything.

'But he can't tell me what to do. And there aren't any other kids on the block my age anyway.'

When she said that, it made him wonder if she would be playing with him if there were white kids around. He didn't want to think about that.

'I feel kinna funny coming over when they leave. I mean it's the first time I've ever really disobeyed them, and some of those nosy people might tell on me.'

'Well, I don't want to get you in trouble,' he said, wondering why he felt he had to take the blame.

'Oh, I ain't worried. What can he do to me? All he can do is give me a whipping and tell me not to come no more. And the whipping won't hurt long and I'll still come. So, he really can't do nothing.'

Allen had never thought of it that way, and when he did he realized she was right. What could his father do to him? *Really* do to him? Nothing. Absolutely nothing.

'Can I see some of your paintings?'

'Sure,' he said.

She climbed over the fence.

'I'll go get them.'

'Can I come?'

'It'll only take me a minute.' Part of him wanted her to see the studio his father had built and his big drawing board, just like the ones at school. But he really would get in trouble if anyone saw her going into his house. He wanted her to see how neat and clean he kept the room too. He kept his sketchpads and watercolor paper on one shelf. On another were empty jars, his brushes, and the watercolor paint tubes. On the walls he put his favorite paintings, not only those he'd done, but copies of paintings by Winslow Homer and Edward Hopper. He guessed Hopper was his favorite. He liked the way everybody and everything seemed frozen in Hopper's paintings. And he had a feeling that maybe that was the way things really were. Things only appeared to be moving or changing, but really they weren't. Like the people he used to watch working in the cotton fields near his grandmother's. All day long he'd watch them, and although he knew they moved up and down the rows with their hoes, they looked the same. And every day it was like that. And every year when he went back they were there. Maybe they were different people, but it didn't matter. It was the same.

Nobody ever saw his paintings except his mother, and he didn't know why he continued to show them to her. She never seemed to like any of them. Maybe if he had a good art teacher in school that fall, he would show them to him. But he felt his paintings were the real him and nobody had ever known the real him. The thought of somebody doing so frightened him. He took her a series of still lifes he'd been working on. He liked vases and jars and glasses. They were hard to paint, but there was something about glass that excited him. Cloth too. He always painted his still lifes against a cloth background, which meant he had to paint not only the glass, but the cloth as it looked through the glass. It was very difficult, but he was proud that he'd been able to learn to do it fairly well. Or so he thought at least.

He walked through the kitchen, where his mother was peeling potatoes. 'I'm going to show Rebecca some of my paintings,' he said pointedly.

'You'd better hope your father doesn't find out.'

He smiled to himself. That meant she wasn't going to tell him, but if his father did find out, she wouldn't defend him. And that was OK with him. Just as long as she didn't tell him.

'Here're a few,' he said, handing the paintings to Rebecca.

'Wow!' she exclaimed. 'They're really good.' She sat down on the grass and spread the three paintings in front of her. 'That's a pretty vase.'

'It's my mother's.'

'And that coal-oil lamp!'

'Oh, I did that at my grandmother's. She doesn't have electricity, and there're all these coal-oil lamps all over the house.'

'I haven't seen one of those in a long time. When Daddy was preaching down in Eufaula, Alabama, we lived in a house that had coal-oil lamps. We put in electricity, though, and only used the lamps for a little while. I never realized they were so pretty till now.'

Allen smiled.

'You paint some funny things.'

'What do you mean?'

'This one,' she said pointing to the last painting. 'I would never have thought to paint a picture of some old mason jar.'

He laughed. 'I like them. They're thick and – and well, I don't know. I just like them.'

'I wish I was an artist.'

'Oh, you can be. Just get yourself some paints.'

'It'd be a waste of money.' She handed the paintings back to him. 'I don't have any talent for anything. I can't even sew. I'm a horrible cook, my mother says, and just plain good for nothing.'

'I bet you could do anything you really wanted to.'

'But there's nothing I want to do.'

He'd never met anyone who didn't want to do anything.

'Oh, I bet there's something.'

'Well, there is one thing,' she said, starting to smile.

'What's that?'

'Play basketball with you!'

She laughed, but he could only manage a weak grin.

'OK,' he said glumly. 'Let me take these back in the house. The basketball is inside the garage.'

When he came back out, she was practicing her lay-up shot. He took a few practice shots, hitting each one. He was determined that she wasn't going to beat him today. She took the ball out first. He moved in to guard her. 'No fair,' she said. 'You're bigger than I am, and play better. You shouldn't guard me so closely.'

'But you beat me. Remember?'

'Luck. That's all that was. Luck.'

He backed away, still determined that every time she drove in for her lay-up, he would block it. When she did, though, he dropped his hands and watched the ball go up, touch the backboard lightly, and drop into the basket.

He took the ball and came down the driveway, dribbling rapidly. She slapped at his arms, squealing excitedly. He dribbled the ball between his legs to get it away from her, but she stayed right with him. She pushed him softly, but he maintained control of the ball and began to drive toward the basket. She shoved him, placing her hands against his chest, and he lost the ball. She laughed as she ran and picked it up and ran toward the basket without dribbling and made her lay-up. 'Four to nothing, my favor.'

By the time the game was over he was angry. She had scratched him once, pushed him constantly, and he wanted to hit her in the mouth. But not only didn't he hit her, he couldn't even bring himself to try and steal the ball from her, afraid that he would miss the ball and touch her hand. So she beat him again.

'What's wrong, Allen?' she teased after the next game. 'Am I too good for you?'

'I guess so,' he agreed. He wondered if she really thought she was better than he was. She knew how well he could shoot.

'Well, I'd better be going,' she said. 'My folks will probably be back any minute. And thanks for showing me your paintings. Do you ever go out sketching?'

'Sometimes, but not since we moved here.'

'You should go over to Peabody College.'

'Where's that?'

'Just a few blocks from here,' she said, pointing west. 'There's the prettiest building over there I've ever seen. It has a lot of big columns or pillars or whatever you call them. Down home we call 'em posts.' She laughed. 'It sits way back and there's all this pretty green grass in front of it. It's almost like a park. I've always wanted to go over there and just lie in the grass.'

'Maybe I'll go over there one day.'

'Could I come?' she asked eagerly.

'Sure. I guess so,' he said, frightened as he heard the words come from his mouth.

'Let's go Monday.'

'Uh – OK.'

'Tell you what. I'll meet you at the corner of 18th and Horton at, say, one o'clock. We can walk over from there. It's only a couple of blocks.'

'OK.' He was glad to see that she wasn't dumb enough to ask him to meet her on her front porch.

'Bye, Allen.'

'Bye, Rebecca.'

The minute she left his stomach started hurting. It always did when he was really scared, and when he thought about walking down the street with her on Monday, his stomach felt like it was trying to grind rocks and glass. He should have told her no, but he couldn't. And it was silly to be scared anyway. All they would be doing was walking down the street. That wasn't a crime, was it? He wouldn't hold hands with her or anything like that. But he knew that that wouldn't make any difference to anyone. He couldn't back out though. Not if she didn't, and he didn't think she would.

He stayed in his studio all that evening, a piece of watercolor paper tacked to his drawing board. But he didn't paint, though he had his tubes of paint, a jar of water, brushes, and a plate of glass on which to mix colors on the small end table next to him. He drew a rough sketch of a tree on the paper, but his mind wasn't on it.

'What's the matter with you?' his father asked when he came upstairs.

'Who, me? Nothing.'

'Wrestling is on TV tonight.'

'I think I'll go in my room and read.' He left the parents sitting in the living room looking at television. His mother didn't watch it much, but he and his father did every night. They'd been the first ones on their block in Kansas City to get a television, and he had been so fascinated by it that when he came home from school, he'd turn it on and sit and watch the test pattern. He didn't care what was on. Sometimes he'd sit and watch the white lines on the screen when even the test pattern wasn't on. So if he wasn't watching television, he knew his father knew something was wrong. Rev. Anderson probably thought he was still upset by their argument at dinner the other day. At least Allen hoped that's what he thought. His mother probably knew it had something to do with Rebecca, though she didn't know he was going out with her Monday.

A section of the text is omitted here. Allen is now return-
ing home late on Monday afternoon...

Allen walked in the back door and through the kitchen. 'I'm back,' he said glumly to his mother, who was standing at the stove.

'Don't go anywhere. Your father wants to see you.'

'About what?'

'You know what.'

Allen didn't know how they could've found out so soon. 'Where is he?'

'He's taking a nap. He'll be up in a little while and will want to see you first thing.'

He went into his room and waited uneasily for the sound of his father's footsteps in the hall. He was afraid to even imagine what his father would do to him. He jumped when he heard the knock on his door. 'Come in,' he said nervously.

His father came into the room slowly. 'You busy?'

'No, sir,' Allen said. His father didn't look angry, but Allen decided he'd use a few 'sirs' for good measure. They couldn't hurt anything.

'I had a visitor today.'

'Who?' Allen asked, trying to sound no more than normally curious.

'Rebecca's father.'

'What did he want?'

'He claimed somebody called him and said they saw Rebecca walking down the street with a colored boy. And he figured it was you. Was it?'

Allen started to lie but changed his mind. He was sure his father knew the truth. 'Yes, sir.'

'I told him it couldn't have been, but I figured it was.'

'We went over to Peabody College and she watched me while I sketched a building. That's all.' Allen opened his sketchbook so his father could see the drawing.

'Didn't I tell you to stay away from that girl?' his father asked, but still not showing any anger.

'Yes, sir.'

'But you got a mind of your own. Is that it?' His voice remained even and Allen had never known him to be serious in this way.

'I don't know, Daddy. I know what you said and all that, but – but, I can't explain. It was just something I had to do.'

'No matter what might happen to you.'

'I just couldn't be afraid of a white girl. That's all.'

Rev. Anderson nodded, as if he understood. 'Well, her father was fit to be tied. He was yelling and carrying on about "Keep your boy away from my daughter or I'll have him put in the penitentiary." I told him if he tried that he'd better be prepared to go meet St Peter, 'cause I'd kill him dead.'

Allen's eyes widened.

'Well, he kinna calmed down when I said that. These peckerwoods are cowards. That's why you ain't never heard of just *one* of 'em coming to lynch a nigger. They got to get thirty or forty together. I told him that my son was a good boy and as far as I was concerned his daughter was lucky that you'd even

36

talked to her, because you didn't talk to just anybody.' Rev. Anderson chuckled. 'Well, he didn't know what to say to that. He come over here expecting to scare the daylights out of me, and when I stood up to him he had to back down. I told him you were a good Christian and he didn't have a thing to worry about. I laid it on thick and he calmed down. He didn't like it one bit, of course, but I don't think he'll cause any trouble.'

Allen didn't know what to say.

'You just be careful. Don't get in a position where anybody can even think you might've been doing something wrong with her. You understand?'

'Yes, sir.'

'Long as people can see what you doing, you'll be OK, I guess.'

Allen couldn't believe that his father had changed his mind. It was too good to be true.

'Anyway, he said that he believes they've found a buyer for the house, and if everything goes through they'll be moving out by the first of September.'

The news hit Allen harder than he would have imagined. He had stopped thinking that one day she might move. But that was probably why his father wasn't too upset. Rebecca would be leaving and that would solve everything. Still, Allen was pleased that his father had defended him. He could've acted like he had with the man in the filling station.

'Well, you better go wash up. I think your mother's about got supper ready.'

Once Upon A Time

Once upon a time, son
they used to laugh with their hearts
and laugh with their eyes;
but now they only laugh with their teeth,
while their ice-block-cold eyes
search behind my shadow.

There was a time indeed
they used to shake hands with their hearts;
but that's gone, son.
Now they shake hands without hearts
while their left hands search
my empty pockets.

'Feel at home,' 'Come again,'
they say, and when I come
again and feel
at home, once, twice,
there will be no thrice–
for then I find doors shut on me.

So I have learned many things, son.
I have learned to wear many faces
like dresses–homeface,
officeface, streetface, hostface, cock-
tailface, with all their conforming smiles
like a fixed portrait smile.

And I have learned too
to laugh with only my teeth
and shake hands without my heart.
I have also learned to say, 'Goodbye,'
when I mean 'Goodriddance';
to say 'Glad to meet you,'
without being glad; and to say 'It's been
nice talking to you,' after being bored.

But believe me, son.
I want to be what I used to be
when I was like you. I want
to unlearn all these muting things.
Most of all, I want to relearn
how to laugh, for my laugh in the mirror
shows only my teeth like a snake's bare fangs!

So show me, son,
how to laugh; show me how
I used to laugh and smile
once upon a time when I was like you.

Gabriel Okara
Nigeria

*P*rivate Eloy

This story is set in Cuba with the Caribbean island under the rule of the dictator Batista. He had come to power in 1952 by a military coup, dissolving parliament and outlawing opposition. Most Cubans lived in extreme poverty. A former student leader, Fidel Castro, and a small group of men and women, began to organise secretly against Batista and by 1957, despite setbacks, they had regrouped in guerilla bands in the hills and were carrying out daring raids. Eloy, in this story, becomes a soldier in Batista's army and the story covers this span of time.

Eloy was born in the valley of Vega Vieja of peasant parents: his mother a hardworking, smiling mulatto woman, his father a hefty Galician[1] who boasted that he had laid more rails in the region of San Juan de Potrerillo than any man on earth. Eloy was the fifth child in a family of nine.

From the time he was very small Eloy knew the land. He was obliged to work hard, from milking-time in the chill of 2am, when he had to take care of the calves, to the hoeing, the ploughing, the selling of the milk in the far-off town. There was not much schooling for Eloy. His mother barely taught him his first letters. His father, an illiterate who could not re-sign himself to his ignorance, lamented the lack of a school in the valley. Often he would say to his wife. 'If the children could only study a little they could get away from this slavery in the fields. Here they'll throw their lives away working and end up with nothing.'

But no teacher came to the valley of Vega Vieja. Who did come were the Rural Police, the pair of them, riding fat horses, receiving greetings and offerings – a turkey, a couple of chickens – from the intimidated peasants watching the police with ancestral fear. And the peddler of clothes and trinkets, he came, and so did the politician full of smiles and back-slapping, looking for votes and promising projects that never came to anything.

And it was one of these well-dressed, two-faced politicians who, years later, noticed that under his rags Eloy had the same robust body as his father and proposed to the family, 'If you get me a hundred votes in the Vega Vieja district I'll get him into the army for you . . . . But fair's fair. You bring me a hundred pledged votes and I'll fix it with the Colonel.'

This promise fell on Eloy's ears like spring rain on thirsty maize fields. It was irresistible. Although the family had some doubts at first, knowing the politician's lying tongue, they finally came to a decision. 'If he gets into the army the boy's made. Not much work and a pay-packet. Free clothes and food and some money to help us out a bit. . .'

But the prudent Galician was not happy about it. 'If you're a soldier you're the lowest card in the pack. You get kicked around by everyone from the corporal to the lieutenant. He won't study at all, he'll just take orders, no education, nothing and he'll probably end up behaving like all the rest. . .'

But nobody took any notice of him. The family rushed out to look for votes and got promises from half Vega Vieja and even further afield. The result was astounding: more than a hundred pledges. The politician was informed, he collected the list and a few days later he was back with Eloy's papers.

He embraced the young *guajiro*[2], handed him an envelope and said, 'Fair's fair. Here's your posting. Take this envelope and report to the headquarters in Las Villas.'

And with more embraces all round he went off very pleased with himself, taking the new soldier with him. Eloy was carrying a little bundle containing a change of linen underwear, a pair of socks, a shirt and a spare pair of trousers. He was wearing a *guayabera*[3] of coarse drill, his Sunday best, and thick trousers bagging heavily at the knees in spite of the shiny starch.

At headquarters he was assigned to Santa Clara barracks. There he made friends among the soldiers, peasants like himself, and adapted easily to the discipline of the job. And he felt happy, proud of his khaki uniform and of the arms he carried which gave him a new authority. He had a sense of his importance and enjoyed his position which had rescued him from poverty and toil with no future but a miserable hut and a thankless struggle with the soil.

To begin with he helped his parents with a few pesos and went to visit them in his new uniform, dazzling his family and the neighbours with his rifle and his soldier's trappings, his shiny boots and his complexion, already so much lighter. Eloy was happy.

But his prudent Galician father asked, 'Are you studying?' 'Not yet,' answered his son. 'That's bad. You'll be nothing but a turnip with a tie on. Well-dressed and clean outside and an ignorant clodhopper inside.'

They laughed and said goodbye. And Eloy went back to the city barracks and carried on just the same, without studying, as he couldn't be bothered with reading, and anyway his life was easy. He knew the value of a peso so he did not waste his money. And he went on helping his parents until he met Eulalia.

His small wages went on her, in presents and taking her out. And one night he carried her off. He rented a room, furnished it sparsely and then Eloy began to feel the pinch. He loved Eulalia and took care that she didn't want for anything.

One afternoon as he was leaving the barracks Lieutenant Valladares said to him, 'You can't go home. We've got an eviction tomorrow in Rio Chiquito.'

Eloy didn't understand what it was all about, but as usual he obeyed. That was the first thing he had been taught, blind obedience to his superiors. He sent a message to Eulalia and resigned himself to the situation.

At dawn they rode out into the countryside. Surrounded by the wildness of nature, the lonely woodland and savannah, with the morning sun shining, the birds singing, the vultures wheeling, the scent of lianas and tender leaves, Eloy felt the joy of his childhood, he was back in his own element. The sun in the open country was doing him good. He rode along cheerfully. He hummed a song.

After six hours' riding they reached Rio Chiquito. There he saw them, at the door of the hut. Their torn clothes, their thin, dry faces, their bare feet, the half-naked children in their arms. Their lifeless eyes. Their silent, pale lips.

The Lieutenant said to them, 'You've got to leave. You're being evicted. . .'

The head of the family replied humbly, 'We don't know where to go.' The Lieutenant answered, 'We're sorry, we really are sorry. But the law's the law. You've got to get out.' An old man said, 'The law is unjust. We always pay the rent.' The Lieutenant replied, 'I've got the legal warrant here – and that's what counts. The land isn't yours and you've got to go. Start loading your stuff onto the cart because we're here to see that the law is carried out.'

Eloy watched the eviction, in silence, disturbed. He saw the thin arms straining to heave the shabby iron beds onto the cart, the wardrobe with two planks missing at the back, the pine table half eaten away by termites, three stools, a cradle with the paint peeling, bundles of clothes, a wooden plough, the stone water-filter, the wash-basin. . .and he thought of his family, thought that the same thing might happen to them.

And Eloy was troubled.

They escorted the evicted family to a boundary of coconut palms and after watching them disappear down a lane they went back to the hut and burnt as the Lieutenant ordered.

Eloy, holding a flaming branch, his face glowing in the firelight, felt uneasy.

On the way back, as his horse trotted along briskly, nature did not seem so beautiful any more. He felt guilty. He thought of the evicted peasants, of what their fate would be in that countryside where work was non-existent. Facing the rigours of the 'dead season'. . . .

When he reached the barracks he felt ill. And that night he found no happiness in Eulalia's arms.

His other disagreeable mission happened during the sugar harvest. There was a strike of workers who were not being paid a fair wage. His detachment arrived in the forecourt of the paralysed refinery. Eloy, together with other soldiers, arrested some workers. He took them out of their houses and made them get into lorries to be taken to the city prisons. He saw them close up, some were peasants like himself. They were justifying themselves, 'We're on strike because they won't give us our rights.' 'Get into the lorry. I don't want any lip from you,' said the lieutenant.

None of the workers put up any resistance against the weapons pointing at them. They climbed into the lorry with an expression of determination. Eloy watched them leave, a twinge of anguish in his heart.

That same day he patrolled the canefields. Rifle in hand, he walked round the boundaries ready to fire at any striker who might try to set fire to the sugar-cane.

The next day, as he was standing sentinel in the deserted

forecourt, a little boy came up to him. 'Guard, mama is ill and needs to go to the doctor. Help me to lift her up. There's no one here. They've all gone.'

Eloy went into the hut and lifted an emaciated woman from the floor. 'She has attacks,' said the child. 'And your father?' asked Eloy. 'He's in prison.' Eloy looked at him uneasily. The unconscious woman sighed faintly. She stretched her limbs and opened her eyes. Eloy quickly asked her. 'Your husband, where is he?' 'He is a striker. He's in prison,' murmured the woman.

Eloy looked at the hut and saw the poverty, the same that he knew so well, the same as in his own hut. He saw the shabby stove with its clay pot, the broken-seated chairs, the beds covered with rags. 'He's in prison,' repeated the little boy.

Eloy was getting fat. He found the life easy. He asked for nothing more. His was a life of simple routine, very different from the heavy labour in the fields where he had had no clean clothes, no good shoes, no money. He would not have changed his status as a soldier for any thing in the world. He knew poverty and its despair at close quarters. Nobody was going to make him give up his uniform and his salary. Not even his Eulalia. Nor his two-year-old son. It was a life without ups and downs. Get paid, follow the routine and live . . . No other ideas bothered him much. Politics or injustices or crimes. He was safe. That was how the world was and he had a position in the world, that of a soldier. And that was enough for him. But every now and then he didn't forget the evicted family and the striker's little boy.

In the world around him, not everything was going well for the government. There had been risings in the mountains against the crimes. Despotism was reaping its natural harvest and now the soldiers were going out to fight the rebels in the mountains. The days were not peaceful any more. The war was a bitter reality which he had to face up to. Eloy was not a coward. Eloy knew how to obey. Eloy went to the front.

Eulalia hung religious medals round his neck. She made him accept a charm to ward off bullets, embroidered by her with the Sacred Heart of Jesus in red to protect him from death. She gave him the Prayer of the Just Judge for him to read and carry with him. And Eloy accepted it with a smile. He kissed his son goodbye and held the weeping Eulalia tightly to him.

Eloy knew that the rebels were fighting a bad government. He said to himself, 'All governments are bad and I've got to serve whatever government it happens to be.' And he accepted his position fatalistically. The world was too complicated for him. 'What can I do about it?' he thought.

His lieutenant went with him to the combat zone, leading his detachment. After six exhausting days' marching they reached their objective. 'Let's hope this will soon be over,' said Eloy to his friend Private Julian, a *guajiro* like himself, while the campaign rations were being prepared in a grove of *yagruma* trees at the foot of a hillside. 'Yes. But it looks a long job . . . . Although they haven't got a chance against us. Not against the army . . .' Eloy smiled, a little reassured. The breeze blew cool through the leaves of the *yagrumas* which sheltered them.

The mountain peaks looked very near. He could make out the vultures flying, high up, like moving black dots against a prussian blue firmament. 'Up there,' he said to himself nervously, 'that's where they are.'

At dawn they began the climb. They went forward slowly. An advance party was clearing the way. Behind them marched the main body of soldiers, in single file, well spaced out so as not to make things easy for the snipers hidden in the forest. Behind every tree trunk death was spying on them. The weary soldiers were well aware of that.

After five hours' march they pitched camp at the foot of a small hill. One of the first spells of guard duty fell to Private Eloy. He took up his post behind a rock, looking out over a valley full of palm trees and mist. In the distance he could see the sea, a fringe of pale blue. His companion on duty said, 'Not my idea of a good time, stuck here in these bushes.' 'Not mine either. I don't know what we're doing here,' answered Eloy. And they both stared at the horizon, looking for possible signs of the rebels.

At nightfall the shooting began. Nobody slept well. Shots that came from nobody knew where. Nervous guards firing. Tense nerves. At first light they continued the weary march, from mountain to mountain through dales and gorges. It was cold and drizzling. A constant mist blurred the trees. Raindrops on the leaves, mud. The soldiers chatted among themselves, 'You can't see a thing.' 'Why aren't we going down yet?' 'Why can't they send somebody else on this wild goose chase?'

At sunrise they came under heavy fire. A group of rebels suddenly blazed away at them. The leading soldiers fell, surprised by bursts of shots coming from no fixed point. Eloy saw them coming back, pale-faced and groaning. The lieutenant, revolver in hand, came up to them. 'Now it's our turn to go on ahead. Forward!' And Eloy moved into the vanguard.

A day later he went into battle. As they were going along a path between tall hollyhocks the bullets reached them. Three comrades fell. Eloy fired blindly straight ahead towards the woods. Beside him the machine-guns opened fire on an invisible enemy: the guerrillas. The lieutenant urged them on. 'Into the woods! They're in those woods!'

The soldiers advanced. At full speed. Before reaching the woods ahead several had fallen to the grass. Eloy arrived. He pushed on into the woods. Rifle ready to fire. But he couldn't see anyone. He went on.

From beside the trunk of a *yaba* tree someone spoke to him. It was a bearded man, very young. He was leaning heavily against the tree-trunk, motionless. Eloy went up to him cautiously. He saw the blood. 'I'll take him prisoner,' thought Eloy. He heaved him on to his shoulders. He didn't weigh much. He was a thin man, his uniform torn and dirty. Eloy walked a little way. He got tired. Carefully he laid the wounded man down on the grass while he got his strength back. He listened. There was no sound of shouting any more.

'I'm thirsty. Give me some water.' Eloy pointed his gun at the man's eyes. But all he saw in them was fever and helplessness. 'Water.' Eloy looked at him. It was a peasant face, like his own, a long-suffering face. The wounded man drank from the bottle Eloy handed him. 'Thanks.' 'That's all right,' said Eloy. And he did not know what to do.

'I think I'm badly hurt,' said the wounded man. 'No, no you aren't.' 'I shan't get out of this alive.' Eloy thought, 'If I take this *guajiro* prisoner he'll certainly be murdered. The lieutenant will kill him. He's already killed two *guajiros* just because they couldn't tell him where the rebels were.'

'How old are you?' 'Nineteen,' said the wounded man. Eloy thought, 'If I take him the lieutenant will kill him. I'll leave him here. Let him take his chance. Anyway he can't live long with a Springfield bullet in his stomach.'

The wounded man looked questioningly at him. He could see him thinking. He knew his fate was being decided. 'Come with us, soldier, come on . . .' Eloy didn't answer. He hesitated. He didn't like the lieutenant and he didn't care for the government. Undecided, he didn't know what to do. 'Come with us,' repeated the young man. 'You carry me and I'll guide you.'

Eloy got up and said. 'I'm going to spare your life, you're a *guajiro* like me. Escape as soon as you can.' 'I can't, soldier, I can't escape. If you go, kill me, I don't want to die here – all by myself. Take me to my people and come and join the revolution.' Eloy said nothing. he turned his back on the wounded man. He walked out of the wood.

'We'd given you up,' said a soldier who was a friend of his. 'They caught us by surprise. There are two dead.'

That night none of the soldiers slept. They were expecting a surprise attack. Eloy, lying awake, thought, 'I'd go, but what about Eulalia and the boy . . . And beginning to face hardships now. When I was all settled in life. . . Poverty in the fields all over again . . . His wound wasn't serious. Wonder if he's still alive? I ought to have killed him really, so he wouldn't suffer any more. But I couldn't have done it.'

At daybreak they were issued with rations. Eloy put aside two bananas, a tin of condensed milk, some biscuits. And at the first opportunity he slipped away into the woods.

There he was, even paler than before. He was delirious with fever. 'Here, I've brought you some biscuits and bananas and a can of milk . . .' But the wounded man didn't recognise him. Eloy said to himself, 'If I carry him now I don't know where to take him. Even if I wanted to go with him now he can't guide me. . .'

He found himself surrounded by rifles. The lieutenant shouted, 'Hang them both! Traitors have to be hung!' Eloy saw the ropes, the noose. He didn't try to defend himself.

When the troop turned and looked back for an instant to see if the two bodies had stopped twitching, they saw them swaying in the wind which blew down from the Sierra.

The lieutenant remarked to his shaken orderly, 'I never liked Private Eloy,' he said, scratching his eyebrow. 'He wasn't a safe man.' The orderly said nothing. They crossed a stream, its waters ruffled by the strong breeze. Its banks were covered with fine grey sand. The lieutenant knelt down at the water's edge and bathed his eyebrow where a mosquito bite had raised an irritating swelling.

1 *someone whose family originated from Galicia in north-west Spain*
2 *peasant*
3 *a loose-fitting shirt*

Small Avalanches

I kept bothering my mother for a dime, so she gave me a dime, and I went down our lane and took the shortcut to the high-way, and down to the gas station. My uncle Winfield ran the gas station. There were two machines in the garage and I had to decide between them: the pop machine and the candy bar machine. No, there were three machines, but the other one sold cigarettes and I didn't care about that.

It took me a few minutes to make up my mind, then I bought a bottle of Pepsi-Cola.

Sometimes a man came to unlock the machines and take out the coins, and if I happened to be there it was interesting – the way the machines could be changed so fast if you just had the right key to open them. This man drove up in a white truck with a licence plate from Kansas, a different colour from our licence plates, and he unlocked the machines and took out the money and loaded the machines up again. When we were younger we liked to hang around and watch. There was some-thing strange about it, how the look of the machines could be changed so fast, the fronts swinging open, the insides show-ing, just because a man with the right keys drove up.

I went out front where my uncle was working on a car. He

was under the car, lying on a thing made out of wood that had rollers on it so that he could roll himself under the car; I could just see his feet. He had on big heavy shoes that were all greasy. I asked him if my cousin Georgia was home – they lived about two miles away and I could walk – and he said no, she was baby-sitting in Stratton for three days. I already knew this but I hoped the people might have changed their minds.

'Is that man coming today to take out the money?'

My uncle didn't hear me. I was sucking at the Pepsi-Cola and running my tongue around the rim of the bottle. I always loved the taste of pop, the first two or three swallows. Then I would feel a little filled up and would have to drink it slowly. Sometimes I even poured the last of it out, but not so that anyone saw me.

'That man who takes care of the machines, is he coming today?'

'Who? No. Sometime next week.'

My uncle pushed himself out from under the car. He was my mother's brother, a few years older than my mother. He had bushy brown hair and his face was dirty. 'Did you call Georgia last night?'

'No, Ma wouldn't let me.'

'Well, somebody was on the line because Betty wanted to check on her and the goddam line was busy all night. So Betty wanted to drive in, all the way to Stratton, drive six miles when probably nothing's wrong. You didn't call her, huh?'

'No.'

'This morning Betty called her and gave her hell and she tried to say she hadn't been talking all night, that the telephone lines must have gotten mixed up. Georgia is a goddam little liar and if I catch her fooling around...'

He was walking away, into the garage. In the back pocket of his overalls was a dirty rag, stuffed there. He always yanked it out and wiped his face with it, not looking at it, even if it was dirty. I watched to see if he would do this and he did.

I almost laughed at this, and at how Georgia got away with murder. I had a good idea who was talking to her on the telephone.

The pop made my tongue tingle, a strong acid-sweet taste

that almost hurt. I sat down and looked out at the road. This was in the middle of Colorado, on the road that goes through, east and west. It was a hot day. I drank one, two, three, four small swallows of pop. I pressed the bottle against my knees because I was hot. I tried to balance the bottle on one knee and it fell right over; I watched the pop trickle out onto the concrete.

I was too lazy to move my feet, so my bare toes got wet.

Somebody came along the road in a pick-up truck, Mr Watkins, and he tapped on the horn to say hello to me and my uncle. He was on his way to Stratton. I thought, *Damn it, I could have hitched a ride with him.* I don't know why I bothered to think this because I had to get home pretty soon, anyway, my mother would kill me if I went to town without telling her. Georgia and I did that once, back just after school let out in June, we went down the road a ways and hitched a ride with some guy in a beat-up car we thought looked familiar, but when he stopped to let us in we didn't know him and it was too late. But nothing happened, he was all right. We walked all the way back home again because we were scared to hitch another ride. My parents didn't find out, or Georgia's, but we didn't try it again.

I followed my uncle into the gas station. The building was made of ordinary wood, painted white a few years ago but starting to peel. It was just one room. The floor was concrete, all stained with grease and cracked. I knew the whole place by heart: the ceiling planks, the black rubber things hanging on the wall, looped over big rusty spikes, the Cat's Paw ad that I liked, and the other ads for beer and cigarettes on shiny pieces of cardboard that stood up. To see those things you wouldn't guess how they came all flat, and you could unfold them and fix them yourself, like fancy things for under the Christmas tree. Inside the candy machine, behind the little windows, the candy bars stood up on display: *Milky Way, O Henry, Junior Mints, Mallow Cup, Three Musketeers, Hershey.* I liked them all. Sometimes *Milky Way* was my favourite, other times I only bought *Mallow Cup* for weeks in a row, trying to get enough of the cardboard letters to spell out *Mallow Cup.* One letter came with each candy bar, and if you spelled out the whole name you could send away for a prize. But the letter 'w' was hard to find. There were lots of 'l's', it was rotten luck to open the wrapper up and see another 'l' when you already had ten of them.

'Could I borrow a nickle?' I asked my uncle.

'I don't have any change.'

Like hell, I thought. My uncle was always stingy.

I pressed the 'return coin' knob but nothing came out. I pulled the knob out under *Mallow Cup* but nothing came out.

'Nancy, don't fool around with that thing, okay?'

'I don't have anything to do.'

'Yeah, well, your mother can find something for you to do.'

'She can do it herself.'

'You want me to tell her that?'

'Go right ahead.'

'Hey, did your father find out any more about that guy in Polo?'

'What guy?'

'Oh, I don't know, some guy who got into a fight and was arrested – he was in the Navy with your father, I don't remember his name.'

'I don't know.'

My uncle yawned. I followed him back outside and he stretched his arms and yawned. It was very hot. You could see the fake water puddles on the highway that were so mysterious and always moved back when you approached them. They could hypnotize you. Across from the garage was the mailbox on a post and then just scrub land, nothing to look at, pasture land and big rocky hills.

I thought about going to check to see if my uncle had any mail, but I knew there wouldn't be anything inside. We only got a booklet in the mail that morning, some information about how to make money selling jewellery door-to-door that I had written away for, but now I didn't care about. 'Georgia has all the luck,' I said. 'I could use a few dollars myself.'

'Yeah,' my uncle said. He wasn't listening.

I looked at myself in the outside mirror of the car he was fixing. I don't know what kind of car it was, I never memorized the makes like the boys did. It was a dark maroon colour with big heavy fenders and a bumper that had little bits of rust in it, like sparks. The running board had old, dried mud packed down inside its ruts. It was covered with black rubber, a mat. My hair was blown-looking. It was a big heavy mane of hair the colour everybody called dishwater blond. My baby pictures showed that it used to be light blond.

'I wish I could get a job like Georgia,' I said.

'Georgia's a year older than you.'

'Oh hell...'

I was thirteen but I was Georgia's size, all over, and I was smarter. We looked alike. We both had long bushy flyaway hair that frizzed up when the air was wet, but kept curls in very well when we set it, like for church. I forgot about my hair and leaned closer to the mirror to look at my face. I made my lips shape a little circle, noticing how wrinkled they got. They could wrinkle up into a small space. I poked the tip of my tongue out.

There was the noise of something on gravel, and I looked around to see a man driving in. Out by the highway my uncle just had gravel, then around the gas pumps he had concrete. This man's car was white, a colour you don't see much, and his licence plate was from Kansas.

He told my uncle to fill up the gas tank and he got out of the car, stretching his arms.

He looked at me and smiled. 'Hi,' he said.

'Hi.'

He said something to my uncle about how hot it was, and my uncle said it wasn't too bad. Because that's the way he is – always contradicting you. My mother hates him for this. But then he said, 'You read about the dry spell coming up? – right into September?' My uncle meant the ranch bureau thing but the man didn't know what he was talking about. He meant the 'Bureau News & Forecast'. This made me mad, that my uncle was so stupid, thinking that a man from out of state and probably from a city would know about that or give a damn. It made me mad. I saw my pop bottle where it fell and I decided to go home, not to bother putting it in the case where you were supposed to.

I walked along on the edge of the road, on the pavement,

because there were stones and prickles and weeds with bugs in them off the side that I didn't like to walk in barefoot. I felt hot and mad about something. A yawn started in me, and I felt it coming up like a little bubble of gas from the pop. There was my cousin Georgia in town, and all she had to do was watch a little girl who wore thick glasses and was sort of strange, but very nice and quiet and no trouble, and she'd get two dollars. I thought angrily that if anybody came along I'd put out my thumb and hitch a ride to Stratton, and the hell with my mother.

Then I did hear a car coming but I just got over to the side and waited for him to pass. I felt stubborn and wouldn't look around to see who it was, but then the car didn't pass and I looked over my shoulder – it was the man in the white car, who had stopped for gas. He was driving very slow. I got farther off the road and waited for him to pass. But he leaned over to this side and said out the open window, 'You want a ride home? Get in.'

'No, that's okay,' I said.

'Come on, I'll drive you home. No trouble.'

'No, it's okay. I'm almost home,' I said.

I was embarrassed and didn't want to look at him. People didn't do this, a grown-up man in a car wouldn't bother to do this. Either you hitched for a ride or you didn't, and if you didn't, people would never slow down to ask you. This guy is crazy, I thought. I felt very strange. I tried to look over into the field but there wasn't anything to look at, not even any cattle, just land and scrubby trees and a barbed-wire fence half falling down.

'Your feet will get all sore, walking like that,' the man said.

'I'm okay.'

'Hey, watch out for the snake!'

There wasn't any snake and I made a noise like a laugh to show that I knew it was a joke but didn't think it was very funny.

'Aren't there rattlesnakes around here? Rattlers?'

'Oh, I don't know,' I said.

He was still driving right alongside me, very slow. You are not used to seeing a car slowed-down like that, it seems very strange. I tried not to look at the man. But there was nothing else to look at, just the country and the road and the mountains in the distance and some clouds.

'That man at the gas station was mad, he picked up the bottle you left.'

I tried to keep my lips pursed shut, but they were dry and came open again. I wondered if my teeth were too big in front.

'How come you walked away so fast? That wasn't friendly,' the man said. 'You forgot your pop bottle and the man back there said somebody could drive over it and get a flat tire, he was a little mad.'

'He's my uncle,' I said.

'What?'

He couldn't hear or was pretending he couldn't hear, so I had to turn toward him. He was all-right-looking, he was smiling. 'He's my uncle,' I said.

'Oh, is he? You don't look anything like *him*. Is your home nearby?'

'Up ahead.' I was embarrassed and started to laugh, I don't know why.

'I don't see any house there.'

'You can't see it from here,' I said, laughing.

'What's so funny? My face? You know, when you smile you're a very pretty girl. You should smile all the time...' He was paying so much attention to me it made me laugh. 'Yes, that's a fact. Why are you blushing?'

I blushed fast, like my mother; we both hated to blush and hated people to tease us. But I couldn't get mad.

'I'm worried about your feet and the rattlers around here. Aren't there rattlers around here?'

'Oh I don't know.'

'Where I come from there are streets and sidewalks and no snakes, of course, but it isn't interesting. It isn't dangerous. I think I'd like to live here, even with the snakes – this is very beautiful, hard country, isn't it? Do you like the mountains way over there? Or don't you notice them?'

I didn't pay any attention to where he was pointing, I looked at him and saw that he was smiling. He was my father's age but he wasn't stern like my father, who had a line between his eyebrows like a knife-cut, from frowning. This man was wearing a shirt, a regular white shirt, out in the country. His hair was dampened and combed back from his forehead; it was damp right now, as if he had just combed it.

'Yes, I'd like to take a walk out here and get some exercise,' he said. His voice sounded very cheerful. 'Snakes or no snakes! You turned me down for a free ride so maybe I'll join you in a walk.'

That really made me laugh: *join you in a walk.*

'Hey, what's so funny?' he said, laughing himself.

People didn't talk like that, but I didn't say anything. He parked the car on the shoulder of the road and got out and I heard him drop the car keys in his pocket. He was scratching at his jaw. 'Well, excellent! This is excellent, healthy, divine country air! Do you like living out here?'

I shook my head, no.

'You wouldn't want to give all this up for a city, would you?'

'Sure. Any day.'

I was walking fast to keep ahead of him, I couldn't help but giggle, I was so embarrassed – this man in a white shirt was really walking out on the highway, he was really going to leave his car parked like that! You never saw a car parked on the road around here, unless it was by the creek, fishermen's cars, or unless it was a wreck. All this made my face get hotter.

He walked fast to catch up with me. I could hear coins and things jingling in his pockets.

'You never told me your name,' he said. 'That isn't friendly.'

'It's Nancy.'

'Nancy what?'

'Oh I don't know,' I laughed.

'Nancy I-Don't-Know?' he said.

I didn't get this. He was smiling hard. He was shorter than my father and now that he was out in the bright sun I could see he was older. His face wasn't tanned, and his mouth kept going into a soft smile. Men like my father and my uncles and other men never bothered to smile like that at me, they never bothered to look at me at all. Some men did, once in a while, in Stratton, strangers waiting for Greyhound buses to Denver or Kansas City, but they weren't friendly like this, they didn't keep on smiling for so long.

When I came to the path I said, 'Well, good-bye, I'm going to cut over this way. This is a shortcut.'

'A shortcut where?'

'Oh I don't know,' I said, embarrassed.

'To your house, Nancy?'

'Yeah. No, it's to our lane, our lane is half a mile long.'

'Is it? That's very long....'

He came closer. 'Well, good-bye,' I said.

'That's a long lane, isn't it? – it must get blocked up with snow in the winter, doesn't it? You people get a lot of snow out here–'

'Yeah.'

'So your house must be way back there...?' he said, pointing. He was smiling. When he stood straight like this, looking over my head, he was more like the other men. But then he looked down at me and smiled again, so friendly. I waved goodbye and jumped over the ditch and climbed the fence, clumsy as hell just when somebody was watching me, wouldn't you know it. Some barbed wire caught at my shorts and the man said, 'Let me get that loose –' but I jerked away and jumped down again. I waved goodbye again and started up the path. But the man said something and when I looked back he was climbing over the fence himself. I was so surprised that I just stood there.

'I like shortcuts and secret paths,' he said. 'I'll walk a little way with you.'

'What do you–' I started to say. I stopped smiling because something was wrong. I looked around and there was just the path behind me that the kids always took, and some boulders and old dried-up manure from cattle, and some scrubby bushes. At the top of the hill was the big tree that had been struck by lightning so many times. I was looking at all this and couldn't figure out why I was looking at it.

'You're a brave little girl to go around barefoot,' the man said, right next to me. 'Or are your feet tough on the bottom?'

I didn't know what he was talking about because I was worried; then I heard his question and said vaguely, 'I'm all right,' and started to walk faster. I felt a tingling all through me like the tingling from the Pepsi-Cola in my mouth.

'Do you always walk so fast?' the man laughed.

'Oh I don't know.'

'Is that all you can say? Nancy I-Don't-Know! That's a funny name – is it foreign?'

This made me start to laugh again. I was walking fast, then I began to run a few steps. Right away I was out of breath. That was strange – I was out of breath right away.

'Hey, Nancy, where are you going?' the man cried.

But I kept running, not fast. I ran a few steps and looked back and there he was, smiling and panting, and I happened to see his foot come down on a loose rock. I knew what would happen – the rock rolled off sideways and he almost fell, and I laughed. He glanced up at me with a surprised grin. 'This path is a booby trap, huh? Nancy has all sorts of little traps and tricks for me, huh?'

I didn't know what he was talking about. I ran up the side of the hill, careful not to step on the manure or anything sharp, and I was still out of breath but my legs felt good. They felt as if they wanted to run a long distance. 'You're going off the path,' he said, pretending to be mad. 'Hey. That's against the rules. Is that another trick?'

I giggled but couldn't think of any answer.

'Did you make this path up by yourself?' the man asked. But he was breathing hard from the hill. He stared at me, climbing up, with his hands pushing on his knees as if to help him climb. 'Little Nancy, you're like a wild colt or deer, you're so graceful – is this your own private secret path? Or do other people use it?'

'Oh, my brother and some other kids, when they're around,' I said vaguely. I was walking backward up the hill now, so that I could look down at him. The top of his hair was thin, you could see the scalp. The very top of his forehead seemed to have two bumps, not big ones, but as if the bone went out a little, and this part was a bright pink, sunburned, but the rest of his face and his scalp were white.

He stepped on another loose rock, and the rock and some stones and mud came loose. He fell hard onto his knee. 'Jesus!' he said. The way he stayed down like that looked funny. I had to press my hand over my mouth. When he looked up at me his smile was different. He got up, pushing himself up with his hands, grunting, and then he wiped his hands on his trousers. The dust showed on them. He looked funny.

'Is my face amusing? Is it a good joke?'

I didn't mean to laugh, but now I couldn't stop. I pressed my hand over my mouth hard.

He stared at me. 'What do you see in my face, Nancy? What do you see – anything? Do you see my soul, do you see *me*, is that what you're laughing at?' He took a fast step towards me, but I jumped back. It was like a game. 'Come on, Nancy, slow down, just slow down,' he said. 'Come on, Nancy...'

I didn't know what he was talking about, I just had to laugh at his face. It was so tense and strange; it was so *important*.

I noticed a big rock higher up, and I went around behind it and pushed it loose – it rolled right down toward him and he had to scramble to get out of the way. 'Hey! Jesus!' he yelled. The rock came loose with some other things and a mud chunk got him in the leg.

I laughed so hard my stomach started to ache.

He laughed too, but a little different from before.

'This is a little trial for me, isn't it?' he said. 'A little preliminary contest. Is that how the game goes? Is that your game, Nancy?'

I ran higher up the hill, off to the side where it was steeper. Little rocks and things came loose and rolled back down. My breath was coming so fast it made me wonder if something was wrong. Down behind me the man was following, stooped over, looking at me, and his hand was pressed against the front of his shirt. I could see his hand moving up and down because he was breathing so hard. I could even see his tongue moving around the edge of his dried-out lips...I started to get afraid, and then the tingling came back into me, beginning in my tongue and going out through my whole body, and I couldn't help giggling.

He said something that sounded like, '– won't be laughing –' but I couldn't hear the rest of it. My hair was all wet in back where it would be a job for me to unsnarl it with the hairbrush.

The man came closer, stumbling, and just for a joke I kicked out at him, to scare him – and he jerked backward and tried to grab onto a branch of a bush, but it slipped through his fingers and he lost his balance and fell. He grunted. He fell so hard that he just lay there for a minute. I wanted to say I was sorry, or ask him if he was all right, but I just stood there grinning.

He got up again; the fleshy part of his hand was bleeding. But he didn't seem to notice it and I turned and ran up the rest of the hill, going almost straight up the last part, my legs were so strong and felt so good. Right at the top I paused, just balanced there, and a gust of wind would have pushed me over – but I was all right. I laughed aloud, my legs felt so springy and strong.

I looked down over the side where he was crawling, down on his hands and knees again. 'You better go back to Kansas! Back home to Kansas!' I laughed. He stared up at me and I waited for him to smile again but he didn't. His face was very pale. He was staring at me but he seemed to be seeing something else, his eyes were very serious and strange. I could see his belt creasing his stomach, the bulge of his white shirt. He pressed his hand against his chest again. 'Better go home, go home, get in your damn old car and go home,' I sang, making a song of it. He looked so serious, staring up at me. I pretended to kick at him again and he flinched, his eyes going small.

'Don't leave me –' he whimpered.

'Oh go on,' I said.

'Don't leave me – I'm sick – I think I–'

His face seemed to shrivel. He was drawing in his breath very slowly, carefully, as if checking to see how much it hurt, and I waited for this to turn into another joke. Then I got tired of waiting and just rested back on my heels. My smile got smaller and smaller, like his.

'Goodbye, I'm going,' I said, waving. I turned and he said something – it was like a cry – but I didn't want to bother going back. The tingling in me was almost noisy.

I walked over to the other side, and slid back down to the path and went along the path to our lane. I was very hot. I knew my face was flushed and red. 'Damn old nut,' I said. But I had to laugh at the way he had looked, the way he kept scrambling up the hill and was just crouched there at the end, on his hands and knees. He looked so funny, bent over and clutching at his chest, pretending to have a heart attack or maybe having one, a little one, for all I knew. This will teach you a lesson, I thought.

By the time I got home my face had dried off a little, but my hair was like a haystack. I stopped by the old car parked in the lane, just a junker on blocks, and looked in the outside rear-view mirror – the mirror was all twisted around because people looked in it all the time. I tried to fix my hair by rubbing my hands down hard against it, but no luck. 'Oh damn,' I said aloud, and went up the steps to the back, and remembered not to let the screen door slam so my mother wouldn't holler at me.

She was in the kitchen ironing, just sprinkling some clothes on the ironing board. She used a pop bottle painted blue and fitted out with a sprinkler top made of rubber, that I fixed for her at grade school a long time ago for a Christmas present; she shook the bottle over the clothes and stared at me. 'Where have you been? I told you to come right back.'

'I did come right back.'

'You're all dirty, you look like hell. What happened to you?'

'Oh I don't know,' I said. 'Nothing.'

She threw something at me – it was my brother's shirt – and I caught it and pressed it against my hot face.

'You get busy and finish these,' my mother said. 'It must be ninety-five in here, and I'm fed up. And you do a good job, I'm really fed up. Are you listening, Nancy? Where the hell is your mind?'

I liked the way the damp shirt felt on my face. 'Oh I don't know,' I said.

TARIQ MEHMOOD

*a*n extract from
'Hand On The Sun'

*Jalib and two friends have been viciously attacked in
the playground of their Bradford school by a gang of
seven white boys, cheered on by a white crowd. Sent
home for fighting, they have been planning with other
black students to get their revenge. The author, Tariq
Mehmood, came to Britain from Pakistan in the early
1960s, attending junior and secondary schools in Bradford.*

Jalib and Ranjit were left alone after the crowd disappeared.
People passed; some were smiling. An old woman fed bread
to pigeons. Jalib's eyes travelled from face to face. 'How could
all these people not know what happened to us?' he wondered.

'What you going to tell your father, Ranjit?' Jalib asked.

'He'll have gone to work by the time I get home. With luck I
won't see him until Saturday. Then I suppose I'll try to make
him understand – and get a beating.' Ranjit's father worked in
a textile mill, twelve hours a night. Ranjit really had no idea
what a mill was. He only saw his father at weekends and then
they usually had guests. His father, when he had the time,
preferred to talk to him about what life was like in India. Once
he told Ranjit about the days of the Raj. Ranjit had heard the
word often but did not understand what it meant. He knew
that the *goras*[1] were in India for a long time, but not why. He
had often wondered if the *goras* were treated, in India, the
same way he and his family were treated here.

'Say hello to your father as you get some *jutian*[2]', joked Ranjit, walking away. It was getting late.

'Yeah, see you tomorrow.' Jalib headed towards his bus

stop, then decided to walk home. The thought of what would happen at home frightened him. His father would shout and beat him. His mother would cry. He would never be able to explain what had happened.

He had been so happy in Pakistan. He saw himself again in the village; the sun was out, he was sitting in the shade of a large tree. He always used to sit there. It was a very old tree. The noise of parrots singing their songs at the top of the tree always amused him. He heard the mullah giving his *Azaan*[3]. He saw his friends playing *guli danda*[4]. They used to swim in a small stream, even though they were told it was dangerous.

The stream was about half a mile from the village. During the monsoons the whole area flooded. Beyond the stream, in the distance, were tall hills, broken here and there by erosion. A railway line ran between the hills. There was a graveyard on the plateau of one of the hills and villagers would talk for hours about who was buried there. It was said that many white men were buried there. This information had always puzzled Jalib; what were white men doing out in the countryside, so far from any major town?

Jalib had spent many hours in the shade of the tree overhanging the cliff by the stream. Older boys would copy the *goras*. They would buy long-tipped cigarettes from the village shop, light them, take a few puffs and throw them away, into the stream, laughing when they heard them hiss as they hit the water. Then they would light another, take a few puffs and watch as it hissed and floated down the stream. This, they thought, was how the white man smoked his cigarettes.

Everyone knew that Jalib would go to *Wallait*[5]. This used to fill him with pride. One day soon, he would think, he would be wandering the streets paved with gold. All the older boys dreamt of being taken out of the poverty of the village. They would burn with jealousy when they saw that the children of those who had gone to England were dressed in new clothes and had money to spend on whatever they wanted. They would talk for long periods of time about how pretty the *maims*[6] were. They thought that *maims* were like *hoors*[7] who spent most of their time wandering around in paradise; far from the existence of women from the village, who sold milk, eggs or other produce, when there was any. Their clothes bore the marks of their poverty; their faces were burnt by the scorching rays of the summer sun.

Jalib's early image of England was inspired by these older boys from the village. Whenever he sat with them, he listened intently to their descriptions of England and the riches it could give. They were awakened from their reveries at regular intervals as a train went past, puffing out clouds of steam and smoke. As it passed, they were silent, contemplating this example of the wonders of the white man. None of them had been on a train, except in their dreams. It always passed on into the distance, twisting through the hills as though in pain. The place to which the train took its occupants, who could be seen hanging on its sides, must be rich, they would think. When the train had passed, they would be alone again, to wait for the time when they could be white men.

'You couldn't spare a few pennies for an old man could you, son?' Jalib was shaken from his thoughts by a local alcoholic. When he had first seen beggars in England he had not believed they were real *goras*. He ran past the man without answering. His father had told him that these people were bad. They were dirty. Jalib could not believe they were white.

He turned fearfully into his street. He passed the shop from which his family bought their meat. The shopkeeper was from the same district as Jalib. Every time he went in there, the shopkeeper would tell him about his father and what good friends they were and that they had been in the same regiment in the army back home. The shop was not like those owned by the English people. Here everything was sold. Meat, sweets, spice, *dahl*[8], almost everything you would possibly need. Just like the big shops back home.

'What have you been up to, son?' On seeing Jalib, the shopkeeper had walked to the front of his shop. He was a big man. He had been here for a long time. Everyone came to him for advice because he was just about the only one in Jalib's street who spoke English. He stopped Jalib and lifted the boy's head to look at the marks on his face. Jalib remained silent, petrified.

'We haven't come here to fight. . .' the shopkeeper said

sternly. Jalib pulled himself free and walked towards his own front door.

He knocked on the door, tears in his eyes. His father came and stood in front of him, towering over him like a giant. He was a tall man, slim, and he looked much older than he was. Jalib looked at his father; his body began to shake with fear.

'Have you been fighting again?'

Jalib bowed his head, his tears falling on the dry step like the monsoon rains on hard earth. His father grabbed him by the collar and threw his small body inside. Jalib crashed into the bottom of the naked stairs – they were still uncarpeted – his head hitting the bottom step.

'*Mather choud*! I work like a donkey to bring you here, to bring you up, and all you do is fight at school!' His heavy hand landed on Jalib's face and drew back to strike again.

'Don't hit him again! For God's sake, don't hit him again!' Jalib's mother ran towards him. Jalib had huddled in a ball and was crying loudly. 'Can't you see he's bleeding?'

His father walked away, cursing Jalib as he went into the sitting-room. His mother carefully raised her son's head and wiped his tears. With her *dupatta*[9] she started to wipe blood from Jalib's face. As she did this her heart beat fast, thinking it might be something serious. A sigh of relief went through her when she saw the blood came from Jalib's nose.

'Is it bad?' his father asked from the sitting-room.

'He's only a child. You shouldn't hit him like that. No, it's only a small cut. His nose, that's all.'

Jalib walked into the sitting-room. His father was sitting on their second-hand settee. Jalib remembered going with his father when they bought it. Jalib had seen many beautiful sofas and had told his father that he liked one he had seen in the window of a furniture shop in town. In that shop, things were set out neatly. Jalib told his father, with pride, where the shop was and what the man in the shop looked like. His father had stared at him and told him he was being silly, that they would not be able to afford anything from that shop for many years. He had patted Jalib lovingly on the back and then taken him to the second-hand shop where everything was piled on top of everything else. The difference between the two shops had left a deep mark on Jalib. His father had argued with the shopkeeper about the price of the settee and when he bought it and left the shop, Jalib remembered that his father had cursed the shopkeeper and called him a thief.

'Jalib, come here.' This was no longer the voice of the man who had struck him.

His mother had gone to the kitchen to make *roti*[10]. His father always woke up just before Jalib returned from school and left for work a few hours later. He worked seven days a week.

'What happened? Who did you fight?' Jalib started to tremble again. He opened his mouth but nothing came out.

'*Gora* again?'

'*Ji*,' Jalib replied, bowing his head.

'Allah!' His father let out a sigh. 'Come here, son.' The smell of roasting chapattis was making Jalib's mouth water. The sound of his mother clapping the chapatti in her hands was heavenly music to his ears. The curry pan was letting its aroma escape. Jalib's thoughts were now on how soon he could get this ordeal over and sit down to eat. His father put his arm around him and said, 'You forget about fighting at school, Jalib, son. You'll be a man soon. Remember your auntie. Have you written to her lately?' Jalib shook his head.

'Do you know why you came here? We want you to be someone. A doctor, maybe. I work like a donkey. I never thought it would be like this. They say all sorts of things to us at work. We just take it. I know you must think we're cowards. But this is not our country. We've come here to work. It's a free country. You can do what you like. We've managed to buy this house. Some day we'll sell it and go back home. You're our only son. I want you to be someone.'

Jalib's thoughts went back to his village. Although he did not now think much about his friends and relatives back in Pakistan, when he first arrived he had missed the company of his friends and the stories they used to tell each other. Before his father came to Britain, he remembered the many times his parents would go without a full meal in order to fill his stomach. How, early in the morning, his mother would set off for the distant hill, returning at the end of the day with a bundle of grass for their only cow.

'Jalib, come and take this food up!' He ran free from his father's embrace and darted down the stairs into the cellar, leaving in his father's arms the thoughts he was having about Pakistan. 'Wash your hands before you touch the food! Don't they even teach you this at school?' his father shouted after him.

Jalib rushed through his food. His head was full of the coming battle. At least this time the whole school was involved in it. These thoughts filled him with a sense of confidence. At last he knew where he stood.

It had been a wet and cold winter morning when Jalib's plane touched down at Heathrow airport. His village was full of stories of how, when one got to the airport, the questions that were asked were so searching it was essential not to make a mistake. And if a mistake was made, no matter how trivial, then you would be returned to wherever you came from, on the next flight. So for weeks before he was due to leave Pakistan, Jalib had been drilled in the sort of questions the immigration officer would ask and what he should reply. He had often broken down and cried from the pressure of his training. His mother too had undergone the same sort of thing. His uncle had done most of the training as he had been to England, spoke English, and had been refused entry to the country.

'What is the name of your father? The full name, Jalib,' his uncle had asked him, over and over again. Jalib had been dazzled by these questions. He could not understand why he should have to be asked these silly questions: he knew the name of his father. So did everyone else.

'When were you born?'

How did he know? Jalib had asked his uncle, who had abruptly hit him. When he arrived in England, he was told, no matter how young he was, so long as he could talk, he was expected to answer every question he was asked. Through tears he had replied that even his mother didn't know the exact date of his birth so how could he? They had chosen a date that he could remember easily, and had written it in the documents too.

No sooner had his plane touched down than he was filled with terror. Perhaps he would make a mistake and never see his father again. Maybe they would not allow his mother into the country. From Islamabad airport the plane had flown into the skies filled with sorrow and pain. The passengers were overwhelmed by an avalanche of sadness, as their loved ones were left far behind.

Soft snow decorated the runways; sparkling snow-flakes drifted down from the skies. Walking down from the plane, Jalib had been convinced that the airport pavements were indeed gold, for the sun had been shining extravagantly. From fear and apprehension, his heart had beat fast against his chest. He had clutched his mother's hand tightly so that no one could take him away. His apprehension had bounced out of his chest and down the stairs.

The tension of the people who had just entered the airport and were about to be interrogated by unscrupulous immigration officers, seemed to suggest that they had arrived at their day of judgement. Their lives hung in a balance and depended on the whim of an immigration officer. One simple little mistake was enough for their dream to end and a nightmare to take its place. Everyone was aware that any one of them could be sitting on the next plane to Pakistan, refused entry and sent back amidst humiliating smiles.

Looking around the unfamiliar scene, Jalib wanted to break off a few slabs of this gold paving and go back to Pakistan. He could not understand why he was having to go through all this fear in order to join his father.

The immigration officer started to ask Jalib questions in Punjabi! Jalib felt that there was no end to the power of the *goras*. They could even talk his language as though it was their own.

A massive sigh of relief had filled him as he ran into the arms of his father, who had been waiting nervously outside.

Jalib had often joked with his school-friends about their earlier experiences, what they had thought about England and what they had found when they arrived. One day Jalib had been just another peasant child. A fortunate one, as his father had gone abroad and his family's immediate poverty had gone with him. Suddenly he found himself part of a system which told him that he was a wog and that he must assimilate into a new way of life and forget his 'backward' ways. At the same time, that system ensured that the education he received wouldn't come in the classroom but in the playground.

At break, they often would laugh hysterically among themselves at the *goras'* stupidity, remembering that when they had first arrived at their junior schools the white children, who had never seen before anyone with a different coloured skin, had pulled their ears, thinking they weren't real. There were many times when white children at Jalib's junior school had tried to rub off his skin, convinced that his skin was dark because he did not wash.

The memories of his arrival and initiation into Britain came to Jalib in his dreams. He would wake up in a sweat as he saw himself flying away from his father in the arms of his sobbing mother. He dreamed he had said they owned two cows instead of, as his uncle had told him to say, one cow and a calf. Sometimes he would talk about such things with other children, but all of them kept some painful memories quiet. They even distrusted each other. Their parents had told them not to discuss themselves and their families with anyone because the police might come and take them away.

Shortly after his arrival in Britain Jalib has asked his father why, if there was so much gold on the streets, they didn't just take a few slabs and go back to Pakistan. His father had smiled and told him that stories of gold on the streets were just a *chak-kar*[11]. There was no gold, only long nights. Jalib should work hard, he said, and become a doctor, or something like that. Then his father could return to Pakistan while Jalib sent him money.

Jalib fought hard to sleep that night but he was haunted by the coming day and its dangers. The memories of his first fight with a *gora* were still fresh in his mind. When he first arrived in Britain, he had imagined that these *goras* were not real human beings but some sort of supermen. Especially when the immigration officer at the airport had questioned him in

Punjabi, he had been convinced that there was no limit to their power. From then on he had lived under the impression that the children of the whites must also be all-powerful. Whenever he had been struck or abused, he had never managed to find enough courage in himself to retaliate.

But one day a white kid had hit him and without thinking much, except that he had had enough, Jalib had struck back in anger. His punch had landed on the nose of the white boy. On seeing a small stream of blood, Jalib had been filled with both fear and wonder: fear, because he was scared that this all-powerful white boy would release his implacable wrath on Jalib and that he could do nothing to save his skin; wonder, because he had never imagined that the blood of white people was the same colour as his own. When he had seen the white boy cry, he had jubilantly laughed, for he realized that the white boy felt pain as he did and did not like it, as he didn't. These memories were just about all he had left of the junior school. All the rest had faded into obscurity. For this was indeed the major lesson he had learnt from his early schooling.

1 *white people*
2 *spanking*
3 *call to prayer*
4 *a stick game*
5 *England*
6 *white women*
7 *mythical women*
8 *lentils*
9 *head-scarf*
10 *bread*
11 *trick*

Back In The Playground Blues

Dreamed I was in a school playground I was about
                four feet high
Yes dreamed I was back in the playground and
                standing about four feet high
The playground was three miles long and the playground
                was five miles wide.

It was broken black tarmac with a high wire fence all
                around
Broken black dusty tarmac with a high fence running
                all around
And it had a special name to it, they called it
                The Killing Ground

Got a mother and a father they're a thousand miles away
The Rulers of the Killing Ground are coming out to play
Everyone thinking: who they going to play with today

You get it for being Jewish
Get it for being black
Get it for being chicken
Get it for fighting back
You get it for being big and fat
Get it for being small
Oh those who get it get it and get it
For any damn thing at all

Sometimes they take a beetle tear off its six legs one by one
Beetle on its black back rocking in the lunchtime sun
But a beetle can't beg for mercy, a beetle's not half the fun

Heard a deep voice talking, it had that iceberg sound
'It prepares them for a life' — but I have never found
Any place in my life that's worse than The Killing Ground

Adrian Mitchell

BEVERLEY NAIDOO

a personal essay, 'Young, Gifted And Black'

'To be young, gifted and black,
Oh what a lovely precious dream...'

I can still hear the bright, lilting voices rising up above the usual hum, shouts and shrieks from the tarmac playground, filtering through large dust-smeared windows of a classroom in north-west London. At least the windows on the first floor weren't decorated with wire-mesh like those at ground level.

Below, the barren grey rectangle which served as the girls' play area was completely hemmed in. Overshadowed on one side by the large Victorian building, it was also bordered by a wire fence separating it from the street, a long dark bicycle shed with the outdoor toilets at one end, and a high wall. All the brickwork, once newly red, had become encrusted with the grime and soot from decades of smoke belched out through surrounding chimneys. Not from the east, however, where – past the fire station, hospital and park – stretched leafy, gardened streets and houses with drives, shrubberies and central heating. No, the culprit chimneys squatted to the north, west and south, above row after row of narrow, tightly packed houses, hugging the factories and the giant industrial complexes which had originally spawned them. The greatest culprits were the factory chimneys themselves – enormous hulks on the sky-line, asserting their dominance even over the air people breathed. Day and night the factories sucked in the parents of the children in the playground.

It was my first year of teaching in a secondary school, having moved from a primary school, and I had actually chosen to come here. The headmaster was a character well-known for his views on equality and opportunity. I can still remember my excitement on seeing the job advertised. 'Teacher required for remedial class. Primary experience an advantage.'

But despite my positive wish to work in this particular school, I wasn't the first person chosen to fill the post. The other two applicants were both offered the job before me... and turned it down. In the course of being shown around the school, we had learnt that the class in question had been through two or three teachers the previous year! I remained undeterred, eager to try out my ideas. I imagined an immediate identity with the students. I too was an immigrant, albeit white. Most of those in the 'remedial' class were black, many having come from the Caribbean as young children, leaving the close-knit warmth of grandparents to join parents (whom they hadn't seen for a number of years) in cold, grey Britain. After the freedom of a largely outdoor life, most of them now lived in rented accommodation, sharing limited space and facilities with other families. I too had left behind a land which at least physically was very beautiful. I had come out of the social ugliness and repression of South Africa. Although our circumstances were so different, I felt I understood something of the trauma those children had experienced in being uprooted. I wanted to work with them. Together we could make it.

I should have gleaned more, however, from the interview about the qualities on which I was being judged. My enthusiasm obviously didn't carry a very high rating. It had way exceeded that of the other candidates and yet each had been offered the job first. I remember sitting isolated on a seat well below the level of a podium on which sat the headmaster and two other interviewers, secure behind a large table. Perhaps my memory has exaggerated the gap between us. There must have been a question mark in their minds as to whether I was 'tough' enough not to be the class's next ninepin. Was I going to be simply another loose link in the school's chain of armour? I couldn't see the problem. To me the fight was to be waged against illiteracy and other evils. My students and I were going to be on the same side. Well, for want of a more reliable candidate, I was employed.

It was on my first day in my new classroom that the head of the lower school entered before the bell rang, for a brief, friendly chat. He was a large, fatherly man and, as I was to find out, not averse to using a fatherly cane.

'Do you know what words you should see inscribed above your door every time you walk through it?' he asked.

'No,' I replied, looking at the faded green paint.

'The words are "REMEMBER YOU ARE THE BOSS". Remember that and you'll be all right. But come to me if you need any help.'

He stayed to introduce me to my class and was gone.

It didn't take me long to realise the way things really were in the school. To my students I was another one of 'them' to their 'us'. To most of the staff, the students were 'them' to our 'us'. The role was ready made and I had stepped into it.

Almost all I can remember of those first months more than seventeen years ago is a sense of struggle. After my naive imaginings had been quickly shattered, I decided not to sink. My priority became to stay afloat. If I could at least stay intact, I would see what I could retrench of my hopes – afterwards.

My mind has the useful facility of throwing a blanket over details of unpleasant memories. Had someone been able to video my classroom behaviour in those early days, I would surely cringe. The two experiences I do clearly remember were to do with my own confrontation with authority. Having discovered that my place was amongst the front-line troops (in a war I didn't want to fight but which was nevertheless in progress) I made two attempts to assert a limited independence.

The first was over my right to wear trousers. It appeared that only the women PE staff wore trousers, but I simply ignored the norm and wore them too. I received some surprised looks and queries, particularly from other women members of staff.

'Hasn't the head said anything to you?'

I waited... with my plan. It was the time of the mini-skirt and over my trousers I wore tops that were practically 'mini' length. If the headmaster expressed his disapproval, I was going to strip off the trousers and say, 'All right! Is this more suitable?'

In fact it never happened. The lower school head called me into his office and told me discreetly that my trousers had come to the attention of the headmaster but he had decided not to pursue the matter!

My second confrontation had a less satisfactory ending. The school had become a comprehensive, combined from an ex-grammar and an ex-secondary modern. Our Victorian building, the lower school, was the old secondary modern, while the upper section used the grammar school building, set well away from us in the leafy, gardened part of the suburb. When it was announced that we were to have a Speech Day with prizes, which I was expected to attend, I was taken aback. None of my students was to receive anything. In the lower school they were already isolated, known in the playground as the 'thickies', the 'dumbos' and such like. All the other classes were 'mixed-ability' except for the 'remedials'. I was doing battle with my students not to accept the label and to upgrade their own expectations. I had already made out that the majority of them were in my class largely for social reasons. They possessed a range of abilities which weren't flourishing and weren't recognised. I had begun to realise that the very way the school was organised – the way they had been isolated into a 'remedial' class – was a major part of their 'problem'. Certainly not lack of intelligence.

So, not deterred by my lowly status, I wrote to the headmaster. It was an honest letter, expressing concern that my students were not involved in the prize-giving. I think I also added that I believed Speech Days were a relic from the grammar school... and shouldn't we be looking for new ways to reward and celebrate achievements in a comprehensive school? I declined the invitation to attend the ceremony.

I was quite unprepared for the response that followed. I must have naively supposed that although the headmaster mightn't agree, his political outlook should at least allow him to listen. Instead, I received an icy visit from the deputy head-mistress – from the Upper School. A rare event down our way! The head was most upset. It wasn't true that my students were ignored. They were simply being cared for in other ways more suited to them. It was a great disappointment to the head that I didn't recognise this. The conversation was not a two-way affair and I didn't attend Speech Day. The following year when the event came round again, I explained that I had a relative from abroad passing briefly through London. That mundane excuse seemed to be more acceptable than my letter of the previous year.

Slowly, as the individual personalities of my students began to emerge, and as we got to know each other better, we began to develop ways of working which I can reflect on now without the sense of shame that shades the other parts. Perhaps it was in reading together and talking about books both they and I enjoyed that we came to share something.

But, just as we all continued to breathe in whatever the surrounding chimneys were emitting, our lives were always overshadowed by bigger issues. Racism was a major one. There were daily examples. Coming from South Africa I had ears and eyes sensitive to the myriad forms of insult and abuse, however slight or casual.

A couple of incidents remain particularly clear. I can still see the intense humiliation and hurt in the eyes of a large sturdy boy, usually well able to look after himself. He had come to school wearing leather sandals and on entering the classroom with a smile, another child had called out.

'Hey you, Zulu!'

Both boys were black and the wearer of the sandals retaliated fiercely, 'I'm not!'

Nothing I said at the time about how pleased and proud he could be – of how he could take 'Zulu' as a compliment – seemed able to remove for him the stigma of the words. He insisted in attending assembly in his socks. So racism eats into the soul.

The other event had a happier outcome. One of my students had come from Kenya to stay with an older brother, while his parents had returned to India. The word 'Paki' could be heard from both white and black students. I recall a group of black students coming into class from the playground one day, absolutely jubilant. On their shoulders they carried the Kenyan boy who was grinning broadly.

'Nanji's done it, Miss! He did it!'

'What?' I asked.

'There were these white boys, Miss. They called him 'Paki' and tried to jump him. But he hit them, Miss! He sent them flying!'

A bond had been forged. Nanji had withstood a racist attack by fighting back. He had been through the fire and become one of the boys.

This brings me back to the words of the song with which I began this reminiscence. It was while I was finding myself sucked into a system and a role with which I had little sympathy, that I first heard these wonderfully resistant lyrics, sung with a rhythm and delight that seemed to defy those high walls, the wire fence, the poky, dirty streets and the factory gate at the end of the road. Most of all the lovely voices defied narrow, twisted minds. I hoped the woodwork master was listening. When I went down to the playground there was a group of four black girls, standing by the bicycle shed, oblivious to stares and comments. Their eyes were shining as they kept up their harmonies.

Their singing, and this particular song, became a regular breaktime event for a while. I can't remember exactly when it stopped. It was some time after it had reached number five in the charts with Bob and Marcia. Perhaps it was when one of the four was sent away to a school for 'maladjusted' children. Somehow I felt she would take the song with her.

*I*ndia

Inderjit is the name. In-Der-Jit if you're English. Intherjeet with the double ees dragged out if you're Punjabi. India if you're a friend.

We were having our first row. He wanted to pay for our meal but I said no, that I should pay because he paid last time. He said he never had been able to stand those Indian scenes where everyone insisted on paying for everyone else and argued for hours before paying the bill. 'We should do what the English do and just pay for ourselves,' he said. I said that's right, so I'll pay this time.

'Women don't pay,' he replied.

'Well this one wants to.'

'This one soft in the head,' his hand ever so gently brushing my hair away from my eyes.

'It should be fifty-fifty,' I insisted, 'you shouldn't pay all the time.'

'I only do it because I know I'll make a profit on it,' and the look in his eyes made mine look away and tighten every muscle in my body to stop the red blush spreading over my face. Oh God! He'll think I'm really naive. What was the saying '. . . be as bold as brass'. 'I think everything should be shared,'

I said looking him dead centre, straight in the eye. 'If I pay for this you can pay for the video film.' His grin spread all over his face.

We were going out together. At last! If you could call meeting in the back part of a cafe, walking 'together' on opposite sides of a street, pretending great surprise when we happened to be at the same place at the same time, 'going out'. We'd say wasn't it a small world and for the benefit of anyone eavesdropping we'd talk as though we hadn't met for years and years and exchange all sorts of news and ask after all sorts of people we'd never met, giving them names like 'gangrene-ganges-wallah', 'nose-picker-nosy-parker', 'Nina-never-been-kissed'. Stupid and childish? Yes it was, but it was a crazy time, a technicolour time, a shifting from black and white to colour TV time, from living in whispers to talking out loud time. I'd read about how love makes people think they're walking on air, sing about stars and sunshine and go around with perpetual Cheshire cat smiles on their faces. Goofy I used to think. Round the bend and bonkers with it.

I wouldn't say I'm in love like, wouldn't use that word, don't care for it. Feels like it's been through all the second-hand shops in town; you never know whose grubby hands have touched it. Even if I can't bring myself to say the word out loud I think I've got all the symptoms. Goldfinger said it to me, but I know he'd said it to all his other girlfriends too.

'You're different, Injun.' My heart used to go all soft and gooey when he called me that. 'I didn't feel like this for the others.'

Would you believe me if I said I believed him?

I'd had my eye on Goldfinger ever since last year when he'd had a big thing with Christine Chambers who sat two desks away from me. Christine was a cliché come alive: white, tall and beautiful with long blonde hair. The opposite of me you might say, if you were inclined to be that unkind.

'Thick as two planks,' my friend Suman used to say to console me. Didn't help. Christine had Goldfinger, I didn't.

I don't know when he first got called Goldfinger but it was

on account of the amount of gold he wore; rings on practically every finger, chains around his neck, a gold watch and it was said even his cigarette lighter was gold. Those who didn't like him, like Suman, called him Fort Knoxious. Hurt me that did whenever I heard it. His dad was the richest Indian bloke in town, owning shops and property all over the place. My dad said you couldn't trust someone like that, they couldn't have made all that money by being honest. 'Why didn't you go to private school?' I asked him once.

'You don't pay for something you can get free. How do you think me old man made his dough?'

Christine caught me looking at him once, and smiled a horrible pitying smile. After that she started taking a really friendly interest in me: dragging me along with them, talking to me about Indian families, inviting me out with them.

'Why're you always with that gruesome twosome?' Suman asked.

'I'm tagged on for effect. You know, like you don't know what's beautiful until you know what's ugly. Right?'

'You're an idiot. You're a manic obsessive. Why don't you try a white boy? Boys are all the same. If you've had one, white or black, you've had them all.' Suman had done all her experimentation last year and was now a self-declared cynic. 'Super Cynic Suman. That's me,' she'd announced. I'd pretended to know what it meant. Wasted all my break searching under S in the dictionary didn't I.

I didn't agree with her. I didn't see how boys could be all the same. And it wasn't as if I had a choice. I didn't think I could ever love anyone except Goldfinger. Sounds fatalistic doesn't it? Like Karma and all that. My mum would really scoff at me if she could hear my thoughts; she says you've got to work for everything in life, things don't come from out of nowhere on a silver thali. OK. So how was I going to get him to stop loving Christine?

Let's be honest I said to my mirror that night, turning my face sideways, up and down, around as far as I could. Eyes, nose, mouth, teeth, cheeks, chin, ears and neck. All the right things in their right places. Put them together and add them up and the total is . . .wait for it folks . . . you're not going to believe this . . . the total is indisputably – Plain-Jane-India! Why didn't they total up to Beauty like Christine's? We do our jobs they said, we're functional, we'll help you eat, talk, breathe, look and sleep. What more do you want? I don't want you sticking out like the Rock of Gibraltar I said to my nose, trying to push it back, so the skin wrinkled like folds on a mountain, or these colonies of blackheads, I said, leaning forward and scratching at them. Suman had offered to squeeze them once and if she hadn't been my best friend for years and years I would have suspected her motives in mentioning them out loud in public like she did, just as we were queuing up for dinner.

I held my breath, sucking in my 'well rounded' stomach and, folding up the excess skin at the sides with my hands, I walked around on tiptoe, feeling tall, curvaceous and glamorous. By the time I'd circled back to the mirror, my breath had seeped out, my hands had loosened their hold and my stomach was back resting on its folds and my heels were on the floor bringing me back to my short square shape. The mirror doesn't lie, and I said I'd be honest.

At the Christmas Disco, Goldfinger was with Precious, her black fingers intermingling with his and I asked Christine what had happened. 'He's into multiculturalism.' She looked at me with another one of her awful pitying smiles, 'Hang around long enough and he-may-even-get-around-to-you.'

He did too.

Suman doesn't agree but I reckon it was going to India that did it. Mum got a letter from her parents saying that her younger brother was getting married. She read it and re-read it and tears started running all over her face and as she wiped them away with her chuni she saw me looking at her. 'Don't you ever get married and go away,' she said, 'thousands of miles away, not to see your parents, brothers and sisters for years and years.' She grabbed for her chuni again. 'Use these Mum.' I shoved the box of tissues in front of her. I know she would have liked me to go round and hug her and comfort her. But I wasn't like that. I was India born in England, ice running through my bones.

She did it when we were eating, that is my dad and I were eating and she was standing at the cooker making the rotis. Dad had tried to English-ize her and get her to make everything beforehand so's we could all eat together. Mum wouldn't have it. Said she couldn't have us eating stale food, only cooked us one meal a day and that was going to be hot and fresh. Slap, slap went her hands, the circular piece of dough growing between her palms, then a thump as yet another roti hit the tava. Sometimes I'd just want to sit and watch her, fascinated by her hands moving in a repeated rhythm, going through all the different movements in making rotis. 'I think I should go to India for Jeeta's wedding next month,' she said as she placed a hot crispy roti onto Dad's plate and continued before the strangled sounds in his throat could become words, 'he's the last one to be married and it's important that one of us should be there.' Her hands and eyes busy rolling out the dough, 'More importantly it'll be Intherjeet's last chance to see a family wedding before her turn comes.' If Dad was surprised, I tell you, I was well and truly stunned. Didn't know what to take her up on first: missing school, taking me for granted, planning my marriage . . . I was that astounded!

Things happened so quickly I don't think I found my tongue till the plane touched down on Delhi airport's sizzling tarmac. I never knew sunshine could be this hot!

I couldn't move, thought my *dupatta* (classier word for *chuni*) had caught in the door. It hadn't. It was caught in Goldfinger's hands. I swear he had even more rings on his fingers than before.

'Hello India,' my heart melted so soft you wouldn't know I had one, 'you've changed.'

'No, not really,' trying desperately to play it cool and wondering if Precious was with him.

'What's with all this Indian stuff?'

'Oh well,' hoping the wobble in my tongue wouldn't come through, 'I'm just India-returned, you see.'

'I see,' and there was a gap because I could see that he didn't really, so I blundered on. 'It's like foreign-returned! That's what people in India call people just returned from abroad.'

'Why don't we go and have a coffee and you can tell me more about it.' This was a chat-up line, a let's-get-together line and this time it was for me, for real. Of course I said yes.

I did tell Goldfinger all about my trip, my words tumbling over each other in my eagerness to share with him the excitement of finding a huge, new, ready made family, of seeing the places my parents had always talked about, of seeing things being done in the real Indian way: like shopping for instance. It was great. You sit in front of a huge cloth-covered platform while they throw rolls of material whizzing across it and it all unfolds and flows like a river of colour in front of you. Getting all poetical I was when he said, 'Shall we go and watch a film on my video? We can get an Indian one if you want. That way we can see a bit more of India can't we Injun?'

I was speechless. It was like on a film when they're all chasing each other and everything starts going faster and faster, speeding up till you think they're all going to crash into one another, when suddenly they all stop, everything freezes. That's how I felt. Frozen. Cut off in mid-sentence.

Did things always move so quickly?

Thump, thump, said my heart, wake up he's asking you again. 'What about the latest Amitabh Bachan?'

'What about another coffee,' I suggested, stalling for time.

'I've got coffee at home.'

'I like the coffee here.' I didn't want to go to his place, it was all too soon, but I didn't want to drive him away. I didn't know how I could say yes and no at the same time. 'Anyway I've got to go home soon.' It was going all wrong, and here I was making it worse. 'A right little good little Indian girl aren't you,' he said. Goody-little-two-shoes I thought. Yes sir, that's me. Step over the line? Not me! Won't even go near it. I didn't reply, concentrating on holding on to my tears, waiting for him to get up and leave.

'Want a sandwich with your coffee?' he asked.

I looked up. This can't be the same scene? He grinned his gorgeous grin and said, 'OK Injun?' before he went off to the counter and I thought it's happening, it's really happening and then the big horrible shapes of Auntie Bibi and Auntie Poonum came looming into my thoughts and I knew I'd have to be careful, plan my defences right from the start, make sure I had my alibis all worked out. I would want to tell my parents myself, when I was good and ready but I could just imagine how they would react to hearing from Auntie Poonum or Auntie Bibi that they'd seen me with a boyfriend, doing all sorts of things that girls like me weren't supposed to: 'Hand in hand sister. In broad daylight.' Auntie Poonum always thought things were worse when done in broad daylight. 'In front of the whole world, sister. Shameless!' Knowing her she'd stir it even more and hint that I'd been seen with every bloke in town '. . .with these very eyes sister', opening them both wide in emphasis.

Love. Infatuation. Schoolgirl Crush. Call it whatever you want but it really does do these funny things to you: everything's bright and sparkling and the dullest things become tolerable; life takes on an excitement it never had before and with each day there's something to look forward to. Mum couldn't believe it when I gave her a huge, big squeezy hug one day and she wanted to know what I was celebrating. I talked to Goldfinger like I'd never talked to anyone else, not even Suman. I felt I belonged with him. If our bodies were getting to know each other then how could our minds remain separate? We talked about white people, about our own Indian society, deciding on those things we liked about it and the things we hated about it. We played Indian music and watched Indian films and he said, 'It's such a relief not having to be a cultural interpreter,' and I said, 'Wot's that when it's at home then?' and instead of giving me a sensible answer like any sensible person would, he started throwing all the cushions at me, but I tickled him into submission and extracted my reply, 'Having to explain every pappadom you eat. Now if you don't let me go . . .' I made a strategic retreat but still got drowned in the cushions that came hurtling behind me.

I felt whole and contented. All the different parts of me, the jagged ends that never seemed to fit, the bits that were

English, the bits that were Indian, the bits that were just plain me, melted and fused together.

'I'm not going to have a dowry when I get married,' I said one day.

'Me neither,' he was laughing at me.

I wanted to tell my parents about him, to share him with them. Then, I thought, everything will be perfect. It was terribly important that it should be done properly, so I was patient, waiting to pick just the right moment. As I'd grown older Mum had tried to warn me: she'd said don't get yourself tangled up – our way is better – love should come after marriage – then you know it's for ever; in this country everybody shops for love like shopping for a packet of cigarettes – before you know it you've finished the packet and got yourself a lung disease – but you're hooked so you have to run off and buy another one. I didn't really understand all that. I wanted to say to her that when everyone else around you is trying out different brands you can't not breathe it in too. I had giggles when I thought of introducing Goldfinger to her as my personal packet of cigarettes and saying, as I turned him around, 'Look he's so safe he doesn't need a government health warning.'

Suman and I were laughing as we came out of Ms Missing-Something's class. Actually she was Ms Turnbull; you know the type: jeans, holey jumpers, skinhead hair and woman earrings. 'Needs to remind herself,' I'd whispered to Suman and we'd both giggled ourselves silly. She was Missing-Something because she used Ms and not Miss or Mrs. The boys had shouted it out to her when she first came. I thought it was unfair but she was one of them 'traditional' feminists, always wearing the uniform of the white feminist, she turned me right off. She held a discussion and debate class for us Young Women. We'd sit around in a circle (ever so trendy), clutching our cups of instant coffee and talk about 'relevant issues'. This time the talking had started off with social conditioning and moved on to the different roles of men and women; I can't remember who first introduced the words oppression and liberation into the discussion, frankly my mind was somewhere else (with Goldfinger), and I wasn't really paying attention. I sure woke up though when 'Dolly Parton' Donna started going on about Indian and Pakistani women (she really did say Pakistani and not Paki. Donna was a 'friend' you see). She gabbled on about how they were more oppressed than white women, kept locked up in their houses, shunted off into arranged marriages, having to sleep with men they'd never met before. . .

'White women do it all the time,' I said interrupting her, 'never heard of a one night stand?'

'Who'd stand Parton for one whole night,' Suman put in, and we were the only two grinning in the stony silence.

'Everybody knows Indian women aren't as free as us.' Parton was prepared to stand her ground, you had to give her that. 'I only want to help.'

'What makes you think we want your help?'

'Because I care for women. I only want Indian women to enjoy the things we do.'

'Oh yeh,' and I counted them off on my fingers, '. . . herpes . . . VD . . . cervical cancer . . . AIDS . . .' I could see Ms Missing-Something looking awfully worried, her feminist and anti-racist badges jiggling on her shoulders.

'How many Indian women can choose their own husbands? You tell me that, and if they haven't got a dowry they can't get married at all.'

'It's like bribing someone to marry you,' said another brave spirit coming to Dolly Parton's aid.

'White women can't get married without they open their legs first.' Good old Suman. Ms Missing-Something stepped in and took over. She was upset though she tried to hide it. She didn't tell us off; we were all supposed to be free to express our opinions; so free that she made sure none of us could open our mouths for the rest of the session, spieling on generally about cultural diversity, respect for others' customs, equal rights, sisterhood and so on.

I guess it was poetic justice that Dolly Parton should inform me of the happy event. Came up to me after the class and asked if I'd received an invitation to Goldfinger's engagement party? I was a bit bewildered, thinking he's got a cheek sending out invites for an engagement party without even having asked me if I want to; I'd imagined I'd make him get down on his knees and ask me the right and proper way. B-l-o-o-d-y H-e-l-l! That really is taking someone for granted. Parton was rummaging in her bag. 'Me dad does lots of business with his dad,' she was saying, 'so they always invite us to their do's. Here it is.' She brought out a real expensive looking card. Covered in gold it was. Naturally. 'The girl's coming from India. Some millionaire's daughter. Fabulously rich. Did you know about it?'

'Course I did.'

I'd talked to him once about why he hadn't gone out with an Indian girl before, and he'd said they were hard work. They wanted to be dutiful daughters in front of their parents, but behind their backs they want to run around and do the same as everyone else. It's not our fault I tried to explain. We love our parents, but we can't cut ourselves off from other people either. And we take all the risks, the boys don't. He didn't agree, he thought the girls should choose, one way or the other. I talked about the parents and said how they were afraid to let their daughters go out because they felt boyfriends couldn't be trusted, a bloke can turn round and do the dirty on a girl anytime he wants to. He shook his head, 'Indian girls want to have their cake and eat it too.'

'I think they're special, they're risk takers. Fighters. Anyway,' I asked, 'is that what you think of me?'

'You? You're my Injun warrior,' pulling me towards him. Corny maybe, but ever so tingling in my bones kind of thing.

My mind is saying something, saying it over and over again, saying to him all the time, saying:

'You want to have your cake and eat it too, too Too.'

*

'Why do you Indians always end your names with JIT?' The way it was said it could have been git or shit. He was shifting around behind me, sliding from one foot to another, shoulders twitching all over the place, hands and fingers moving on an invisible instrument. I turned back to my locker to finish putting away my books. 'It's a boy's name isn't it?' He'd shifted round to the side, the little stone in his earring winking at me.

'W-i-c-k-e-d! An Indianologist. My lucky day.' I closed the door, turned the key and bent down to pick up my bag, almost headbanging into his yellow hair as he contorted towards me, his spiky eyelashes centimetres from tangling with mine. I gave him a look that should have blasted him through the wall.

'Why've you got a boy's name?'

'Unisex.' Hiking my bag onto my shoulders I made for the door. He was a kangaroo now, jumping from one spot to another following me.

'Since when did you lot get into the twentieth century?'

'Since about six hundred years ago.' I was at the door now, and trying to get through and close it all at the same time so's he wouldn't be able to follow me. Of course it swung back and nearly hit him in the face. 'Remember,' I reminded myself, 'never say sorry.'

'Miaow, miaow,' nails scratching at my neck. Slipping my bag to my hand I swung it round, putting my whole weight behind it. I couldn't bear to be touched, it was like he'd pulled a light switch and lit up all the things I'd been trying to hide. My bag sliced through the empty air and he was laughing, leaning against the wall, hands in his pockets.

'One day I'll let you hit me,' he said.

'Wouldn't want to contaminate myself.'

'Heavy doors, those. Could do someone a real injury.' He was walking beside me, human walk.

'I'm working on it.'

'Lovable bit of sunshine aren't you. What's with all this Indian stuff?' lifting my dupatta and letting it slip through his fingers. I tore the dupatta away from him, but suddenly I couldn't move, those words again, like glue on my brain.

'Just stepped off the boat have we?'

I turned and walked on, and suddenly he was a dog, yapping round my heels, making pitiful barking sounds.

'Sorry.'

'People are always saying sorry.'

'Sorry?'

'Doesn't change a sodding thing.'

He drew his breath back in horror. 'Wash your mouth out! Detergent. Bleach. Fairy Liquid – softens the toughest tongue. Didn't mean that you know,' face wrinkling for forgiveness like a dog that knows it's done wrong. 'Just a joke.'

'You talking about yourself?'

'Actually,' straightening up and looking human, 'I'm terribly interested in Indian culture.'

I sighed. Should have seen it coming. 'Well I ain't.'

'Then what you wearing those clothes for?'

'Listen you reincarnated missionary. This isn't the tropics you know. Can't run around naked in sub-freezing temperatures.'

'Did you get them in Bombay or Delhi?'

Mi-gawd! A man of the world. I was overcome with admiration. 'Got them down the bleedin market – goin cheap.'

'Like you?' Looked ever so pleased with himself.

'Missionary turned flesh trader. Figures.'

'Only in female flesh,' and immediately did his kangaroo jump, way back, backwards. 'Only another joke. Didn't mean it,' eyes on my bag, hip hopping out of range.

This time last year I would have walloped him one for saying that. Being older and wiser I thought 'he speaks truth who speaks in jest'. (No. I didn't make it up, came from one of my Eng. Lit. books.) And now he's going to say sorry.

'Sorry. Hope you're not hopping mad about it. See you around,' hopping out of sight round the corner.

'Who's the boyfriend?' Suman had come up behind me.

'Clean out your contact lenses huh. That was no boyfriend, that was an animal.'

Suman shrugged her shoulders. 'Same thing. Fancy you?'

'Fancies himself.'

'Did he try the "I'm really interested in Indian culture" line?'

'Yeh, and slipped in Bombay and Delhi like he'd lived there all his life,' we collapsed into helpless giggles.

'Next time he'll talk about integration.'

'Soften me up.'

'Reckon he's a culture vulture? Collecting material for his dad's book on Asian girls.' That had actually happened to

Suman. We laughed so hard our stomachs hurt.
   'He's not even a culture vulture, he's just a filthy lecher.'
   'Wow! Now who's a cynic?'
   Yes. I am cynical now.

Wouldn't you be?

A Tanned Version

And there is a huge immeasurable distance between us,
Between me and them.
They close their minds,
Ask the same repetitive questions,
Arranged marriages, strictness, trousers,
Same order.
Wherever I go.
What will they ask next:
Do you sleep, do you eat, can we touch?
I'm only a different colour
A tanned version of you.
They think we're all stereotypes
Carbon copies of each other.
We don't think they're all Princess Diana.
They're always amazed
When I can talk, can answer, have a mind,
As if to say this one's clever,
What other tricks do you do?
I'm not so very different
Just a tanned version of you.
How come I have to fight so hard
When you just have to show your face?

Hummarah Quddoos

Looking

When you look in my eyes
Will you read the pain,
Will you see the struggle
Or will you judge superficially
From the colour of my skin
The shade of my dress
And forget I have a core?

Hummarah Quddoos

True Grit, Hard Graft

During the 1984/5 Miners' Strike in Britain whole families became involved in the campaign to stop pit closures and to save mining communities. Television and newspapers focussed mainly on the actions of the miners themselves and their wives. However, as this piece shows it was impossible for young people not to become involved as well, developing their own strong political views. Dawn Newton lived in Yorkshire and was fifteen at the time of writing this piece which she originally called 'Why did we fall apart and how did we come back together?'

It all started about a year ago. The atmosphere in the house was cheerful and happy as usual. As March 1984 approached, my dad began to bring up his occupation in most conversations. Often while I was reading in bed at night I would hear the more private conversation between my mum and dad. They never did mention much to me about it, but as the time drew a lot nearer I was soon to be in for a mighty shock. Truthfully it was more like a blow to the head. Yes of course I'm talking about the strike. The Miners' Strike of 84/85.

The first few months were all right. Well, with the exception of margarine instead of butter (one thing I noticed straight away) things all seemed to be running smoothly. My dad had just got his allotment and was planting vegetables. These vegetables on a small plot of land became the essential protein in our diets for the next twelve months. The year my dad was striking seemed a never-ending nightmare. About the first two months I didn't really think about it any other way, only that I was proud that my dad and all the other miners would make sacrifices to save pits and thousands of jobs. What followed changed my opinion. Hundreds of news reports, interviews with a man named Arthur Scargill. A year or so ago anyone who said to me, 'Do you know Arthur Scargill did so and so the other day?' I would probably have said, 'Arthur what? Who's he?' But this made me realise Arthur Scargill, although he failed this time, is a man of bloody steel. It's made me more aware of politics. A while ago I would have rather turned to a Beano or watch Playschool than sit and listen to 'her': 'her' being Mrs T, Mrs Thatcher the so-called 'Iron Lady'. While the situation with the strike was on, I was glued to the little square box. Even if I was to jeer and contradict I'd listen with interest.

The most distressing parts in our family were the pain, the arguments and my selfish guilt. I got my so-called nickname 'Dawn the wanter' ages ago. It was because nearly every day I'd say to mum, dad or anyone in earshot, 'I want this', 'I want that'. My dad replied many times with, 'You'll get some of this if you don't shut up'. I retreated nervously as he had up his fist. Before the strike our family got on okay, but 'okay' is only the word to describe it. I mean I couldn't say we all got on fantastically as I'd be a born liar, what with my brothers, one of who is twenty-seven, unemployed for five years, and the other is thirty, working and getting along fine. They didn't speak to each other for five years after a personal argument leading to a vicious fight. I call myself selfish because I never took no notice of the fact that my brother was getting more depressed each day. After about seven months of the strike I did, as we all did, get concerned, for my brother turned to alcohol to solve his problems. This was then followed by continuous drinking and by a nervous breakdown and a hospital bed in a ward for alcoholics. Several visits were made by a psychiatrist as no way would he go to that hospital, he refused to go. Partly I don't blame him. He's so full of knowledge and is very intelligent. He usually now reads and passes time in the library. Fortunately now after sleeping tablets and valium have been fed into his system he's calmed down and off the tablets and almost certainly recovering. He gets depressed, but in moderation as each and every one of us do.

Mum, she's great, a cheerful person with so much patience. I take after her for that. She's cooked up some gorgeous meals and almost led us to believe we were eating caviare and then steak. Underneath her happy smile there's a woman who's suffering badly, in pain constantly. For my mum has bad arthritis to the spine. She must wear a surgical corset. So I've been helping as much as I can, cooking, cleaning, joking. When mum and me go shopping I see her face frown, the tired eyes dreaming, as at the checkout she sees the woman in front spending fifty or sixty pounds on shopping. I could cry as she looks at the half-empty trolley and the ten pound note in her hand. I'd love her to be happy. Luckily my boyfriend cheers my mum up so much. He is only on a YTS and earning fifty pounds a fortnight. Automatically twenty-five pounds goes to his mother, ten in a deposit account, five for club money and five to his dad which is money he has to borrow. What a life, but still he practically bought me my fifth year uniform. He's a brilliant person and he is very special, not just to me, to us all.

Dad did go out a lot before the strike. He often went for a drink but after the strike he had to settle for homebrew kits. These died down and he eventually had to do with nothing. This made him moody, stroppy and, as the money ran out, very irritable. My other brother works at Danish Bacon. He's bought mum lovely things. Not clothes or a bottle of wine nor cigarettes – my mum doesn't drink, smoke or dress up and she rarely goes out anywhere. But he brings her whopping cuts of meat – beef, pork and lamb, chickens and such. I never ask. I never ask for anything now. My sisters are great too. All three are happily married with children, one blessing at least. They bring us lovely food too, chocolate chip cookies, a change from boring plain ones. My favourite too – wholemeal bread. I hate white packaged bread, why it tastes more like putty.

Me, I've changed. I've realised money isn't everything in this world. Okay it's quite something to be rich and never short, but when you do go short you'll know happiness and love can never be bought.

The worst thing was school. I had to go on listening to stupid girls saying, 'The strike's pathetic', 'I don't know what they're striking for' and, 'I'm sick of hearing about it.' If only they knew the atmosphere in my house, it was so icy you could cut it with a knife. Also when they talk about the lovely clothes, computers, bikes and money they got from their parents for Christmas, I could have cried. More than likely I was crying inside, crying because for Christmas there were not lovely clothes, leather coats and no this and that for me. I could have ripped their eyes out with jealousy. But I had a better present than them all. I had love and comfort from my boyfriend and my family. The little I got from relatives was far better than any clothes and computers. I got a feeling I was needed and my help was appreciated. I can understand any mining family and I know now what it must be like for any one-parent family. The fear and the pride being torn from you like when you have to enter the education welfare office for a coat. I felt like a scrounger and after I came out of the office I cried, I cried violently. My mum too was upset to see my unhappiness, my torturous torment, her upset thinking somehow my career would be ruined. No, not me I'm afraid, I've got determination, I've got the push to do and be what I want. I will get somewhere, I know, even if I have to start at the bottom. Some day I'll repay my parents the kindness I owe them. I'll return something to my boyfriend to whom I owe so much for keeping me going, keeping me fighting.

Now the strike's over there's no time for rejoicing, just the bills, the rent, the hundreds of pounds we owe, almost reaching four figures. My teenage years won't be fancy free, but all down to the true grit, hard graft. But believe me I'm not the sort of person to give in and I swear to god I won't.

Lerato Nomvuyo Mzamane
Homecoming

For my sister Nonkosi;
My cousins Zolelwa and Lebogang;
And for the youth of South Africa,
who will be Azania's leaders,
and history makers.
For Pule.

I was born at Teyateyaneng Government Hospital at Teyateyaneng, a small town (or is it a big village?) not far from Maseru, the capital of Lesotho, of a Sotho mother and a Xhosa father. All I know of my early days comes from hearsay, but I recall very wonderful years whose pleasure was enhanced by living with my paternal grandparents at one stage and my maternal grandparents at another–of course they spoilt me rotten! My paternal grandmother died in 1973 from pneumonia and, according to my aunts, I fretted for quite some time–and why not? After all, when I was born, she immediately nicknamed me Matikoti, shortened to Tiko, because of my tiny structure; then embarked upon 'operation feed my grandchild' and fed me assorted baby's milk and porridges, not to mention the fat cakes, chips and other junk foods my aunt used to provide behind her back. My maternal grandmother died in 1978 from a heart attack. I never really knew either of them, but throughout the years, my fondness for them has soared to great heights and my fear and deadly respect for pneumonia and heart diseases has reached ever greater heights.

My family is what could be called 'modern nomads'. The

earliest journey I can recollect is when we moved from Maseru to Gaberone (Botswana) in 1976, shortly before the Soweto Uprising. In 1979 we were packing again for Aberystwyth (Wales) which we left for Sheffield in 1980. In 1982, my brother, sister and I, aged eleven, six and almost thirteen, respectively, were put on yet another plane and going to South Africa. My parents called it a 'reorientation programme' – we had become African children speaking English with a Welsh accent and whose musical tastes centred around punk rock and heavy metal, not to mention our increasing inability to speak our mother tongue. I can see what they meant.

I called it 'Homecoming'.

I didn't dislike my years in the United Kingdom. I loved Wales dearly and sometimes seemed more Welsh than the Welsh themselves. I loved the little old ladies who sat along the beach across our flat (we lived in an eight bedroom house until the British winter and central heating taught us the facts of life). I loved the quiet dignity with which they would teach me Welsh and tell me about the war, their lost loves and broken dreams (I must have started hating Hitler around this time). I loved the pier and its amusements and how on lucky days I'd add two pence into a slot machine and come out with a pound (unlucky days will not be mentioned for obvious reasons). Most of all, I loved the greenness of the vegetation. My most treasured memories arise from the spring and summer picnics by the streams situated on the outskirts of Aberystwyth.

Sheffield and I never hit it off too well. I'm not sure if I should blame city life – I've always preferred quiet, peaceful places. Sure I enjoyed the numerous parks, cinemas, restaurants and appreciated the Yorkshire Moors, but the English seemed so rigid and conservative compared to the warm-hearted Welsh. However, I managed to become part of it all, although when I look back, I realise that most of it was pretence. I mean, I ask myself what I ever saw in Adam Ant's hit single 'Prince Charming', when neither Adam, the song, or price was charming. Rod Stewart was a phenomenon. Shakin' Stevens' jeans were fascinating. Madness lived up to their name and Toyah was incredible!

Anyway, so there we were, leaving the United Kingdom and flying to South Africa. We were over the moon – not literally since the pilot did say we were cruising at an altitude of three thousand feet. Our first and last stop was Nairobi (Kenya). I remember the enormous and very impressive mountains of the East African Rift Valley, running across the land, as far as the eye could see. I also remember feeling particularly elated even as my brother verbally weighed our chances of survival if the engines would mysteriously cease to function. Kilimanjaro I loved as an observer, not as part of it after an airplane crash. The most tedious part of the journey was convincing my sister Kosi that the pilot just could not turn back the plane and return her to Mum and Dad. She was not convinced.

After a few days in Nairobi, we were on our way home. As the plane landed, the three of us could contain ourselves no longer. We chatted loudly and upon reaching the airplane door tried to squeeze out all at once. It is very difficult adequately to express our feelings as realisation hit us... YOU ARE HOME, it yelled from all around us. You and I know about home being where the heart is and about home being sweet, but do you know of a deep intense feeling of belonging? Of being able to let the whole world know that this is *your* home and to have the echo of your voice ringing beyond the universe? Yes, you belong.

We stopped on the tarmac and only Kosi prevented me from kissing the ground on all fours – Pope John Paul II style! She was worried about her doll, Masai, who was wearing British autumn wear on a warm South African spring morning. Masai sat in her pushchair unruffled, with one eye drooping – the mother never got round to taking her to the optician.

After the fuss of passport control, we then went to meet Tat u'Joe. Sincerely speaking, we were unprepared for the sight that met us. At first I thought that half the township had come to meet us, but upon looking closer at the mob of shouting, shrieking, crying, jubilating people, I saw it were my aunts, Nonkosi and Nomvuyo, a distant cousin, Tiny, a younger one Zolelwa, and Tat u'Joe . Amidst the chaos, I heard Tat u'Joe quietly whisper, 'Happy Birthday, Tiko girl!' My whole being shook with the sheer wonder and happiness I felt. He had remembered! It was September 9th, 1982.

We left the airport and headed for Kwa-Thema, the black township of Springs (analogically like Soweto is to Johannesburg). The excitement still hadn't left any of us; for me it was rising with each minute.

Our first stop was Springs. I remember us walking down the street and my nostalgic pleasure at seeing familiar shops – Jet, Checkers, Pick 'n Pay, Foschini, Ellerins, O.K. and others. As we walked, I asked my aunt for the ladies' room. She took me to the public toilets at the station.

There were two buildings. One was painted cream white and its gloss glistened under the spring sunshine. The other was built of red bricks and had dark stains near the water tank, where dripping water had engraved its presence over the years. The two buildings were across the road from each other – like two warriors weighing each other up and yet prolonging the attack. I immediately walked towards the glossy building.

'And where are you going?' enquired my aunt.

'To the toilet,' said I.

'You are black. *That* is your toilet.' She pointed to the red one whose unpleasant odour I was just beginning to perceive. It was clear it wasn't cleaned too often, if ever.

'No. I want the nice, clean one,' I persisted.

'The nice, clean one is for white people, that one is for black people.' She indicated my skin and pointed at a huge board outside the cream white building.

'But...'

'You are now in South Africa, Tiko,' she announced in a resigned fashion. I looked at her for several seconds, digesting her words.

My deep, intense feeling of belonging developed wings and flew out of the window.

*I*f Someone Were To Ask Me...

These three poems were written by the author at the age of fourteen on a visit to South Africa.

Grandad

If someone were to ask me what
    it's like to visit Robben Island I
    would tell them to ask another
    question
If someone were to ask me what it's
    like to visit a relation who has
    already done twenty-one years
    in prison, and is looking at the same
    again
I would tell that person the visiting
    room is a wide corridor split down
    the middle with a thick, sound-proof
    wall, there are fourteen cubicles and
    you look through a tiny double
    glazed window with a movable
    steel plate in the middle
I would tell that person that the
    way you talk is through a telephone
    with a warder listening in

I would tell that person that they will
    run out of things to say after three
    minutes and it's embarrassing when
    you've waited a year to see the person
If someone were to ask me what it
    feels like to sit on a hard bench and talk for three hours
    down a phone
I would tell that person that when
    they leave they will want a wheelchair
    as the whole experience is extremely
    physically and mentally tiring
I would tell that person that after
    having a telephone receiver pressed
    hard against an ear for two hours
    your arm turns to jelly and your
    ear feels like it's got a hundred
    pounds hanging from the lobe
And then, after telling that person what
    it's like
I would tell that person that the only
    thing you can feel coming off a
    seventy-two year old who's nearly
    spent a quarter of a century behind
    bars is strength
Strength radiates from behind his thick glasses
Strength radiates from his arthritic hands
Strength radiates from his grey hair
Strength radiates from his jaw line
Strength radiates from his soul
Strength radiates

Shanty Town

If someone were to ask me what it's
    like to visit a place like Crossroads
I would tell that person that before they
    go they must cover themself from head

to foot with insect repellent for otherwise
    they will leave covered in large, scarlet, sore, bites
I would tell that person that snow shoes
    would be better as the ground is soft and hard to walk on
I would tell that person not to go near
    midday as the heat of the sun gets unbearable
I would tell that person to go in a van
    because after five minutes they will
    want something to lean against and
    nothing is stronger than a cardboard box
I would tell that person to go to the
    toilet first as toilets are no more than
    a ditch covered by a plank with a
    hole in it
I would tell that person to take a
    good hard sniff of ammonia first because
    the smells are enough to make you
    puke if you feel a bit ill already
I would tell that person that KTC is
    an illegal camp where the people still
    pay rent to the council
I would tell that person that Crossroads
    is a place where the corrugated
    iron huts reflect so the whole area
    becomes one big oven
After telling that person about the heat,
    the smell and the insects
I would tell that person that when
    they hear about riots in the camp
    they aren't just riots for food, or water,
    or decent homes
The riots are because the camp has
    two majors; one that the government
    accepts, and one elected by the camp
    that the government won't recognise
The riots are between supporters of the
    two majors
So, after telling that person about the
    hardship the peoples of Crossroads

endure
After they have gone five long miles
    into Cape Town for a lousy job
After they have spent the day's wages
    on ten loaves of bread
After they have rebuilt a hut because
    the police have knocked their area
    flat
When the peoples of Crossroads get
    back they can still think politics!

South Africa

If someone were to ask me what
    it's like to visit South Africa
I would tell that person South Africa
    is a huge place where at one
    end of the spectrum sits great
    beauty, and at the other, immense
    horrors
I would tell that person Cape Town
    is one of the most beautiful
    places I have ever seen, it has
    a city centre like a mini New
    York, and wherever you stand
    you can see Table Mountain
I would tell that person that sunset
    in the 'homelands' is amazing,
    the sky is streaked with red
    and mud huts sit on the
    horizon just like in the films
I would tell that person how if you
    stand just outside Johannesburg
    you can see how the city just pops
    up from the houses spread
    all around
I would tell that person how for a

mere two rand (one pound) they
can go down an old gold mine
and at the end try to pick up
a full ingot of solid gold
I would tell that person about
the rolling green mountains of
the Transkei
If I were someone who worked in a
tourist bureau and I did not have
a conscience to humanity
I would not tell you about the areas
around Cape Town you cannot go to
unless you have a pass, and unless you're
black
I would not tell you about the tiny
huts which contain one or two
families, in which no one is a wage
earner
I would not tell you about the ghettoes
of Soweto where you can't go without
a pass, and where the residents
have to travel every day into Jo'burg
on the off chance of a lousy job
I would not tell you how black miners
only make enough money for a loaf
of bread each day and are only
employed for eleven months a year
so they don't become citizens
But I don't work in a tourist bureau,
my name is Manelisi, and I have
links that connect me with South
Africa, and most important to me is I
feel for the twenty million oppressed in
South Africa, and the rest of the
world
As Manelisi I must tell you about
when Nzwaki held an ice lolly wrapper
in her hand and looked at a bin
that said 'Keep Your Country Tidy'

she dropped the wrapper on the
floor next to the bin saying
'What country? I have no country.'

ROBERT SWINDELLS

An extract from
'Brother In The Land'

BEFORE

East is East and West is West, and maybe it was a difference of opinion or just a computer malfunction. Either way, it set off a chain of events that nobody but a madman could have wanted and which nobody, not even the madmen, could stop.

There were missiles.
Under the earth.
In the sky.
Beneath the waves.
Missiles with thermo-nuclear warheads, enough to kill everybody on earth.
Three times over.

And something set them off; sent them flying, West to East and East to West, crossing in the middle like cars on a cable-railway.

East and West, the sirens wailed. Emergency procedures began, hampered here and there by understandable panic. Helpful leaflets were distributed and roads sealed off. VIPs went to their bunkers and volunteers stood at their posts. Suddenly, nobody wanted to be an engine-driver anymore, or a model or a rock-star. Everybody wanted to be one thing: a survivor. But it was an overcrowded profession.

The missiles climbed their trajectory arcs, rolled over the top and came down, accelerating. Below, everyone was ready. The Frimleys had their shelter in the lounge. The Bukovskys favoured the cellar. A quick survey would have revealed no overwhelming preference, worldwide for one part of the house over the others.

Down came the missiles. Some had just the one warhead, others had several, ranging from the compact, almost tactical warhead to the large, family size. Every town was to receive its own, individually-programmed warhead. Not one had been left out.

They struck, screaming in with pinpoint accuracy, bursting with blinding flashes, brighter than a thousand suns. Whole towns and city-centres vaporized instantly; while tarmac, trees and houses thirty miles from the explosions burst into flames. Fireballs, expanding in a second to several miles across, melted and devoured all matter that fell within their diameters. Blast-waves, travelling faster than sound, ripped through the suburbs. Houses disintegrated and vanished. So fierce were the flames that they devoured all the oxygen around them, suffocating those people who had sought refuge in deep shelters. Winds of a hundred-and-fifty miles an hour, rushing in to fill the vacuum, created fire-storms that howled through the streets, where temperatures in the thousands cooked the subterranean dead. The very earth heaved and shook as the warheads rained down, burst upon burst upon burst, and a terrible thunder rent the skies.

For an hour the warheads fell, then ceased. A great silence descended over the land. The Bukovskys had gone, and the Frimleys were no more. Through the silence, through the pall of smoke and dust that blackened the sky, trillions of deadly radioactive particles began to fall. They fell soundlessly, settling like an invisible snow on the devastated earth.

Incredibly, here and there, people had survived the bombardment. They lay stunned in the ruins, incapable of thought. Drifting on the wind, the particles sifted in upon them, landing unseen on clothing, skin and hair, so that most of these too would die, but slowly.

Most, but not all. There were those whose fate it was to wander this landscape of poisonous desolation. One of them was me.

AFTER

It was about three weeks after the bomb. A lot of the food and stuff which had been lying in houses had gone. Hunger-pains roused people from their stupor and they began asking when the help they'd been told to expect was going to materialize. Fights broke out, as those lucky enough to find food were set upon by their less fortunate fellows.

The situation was getting nastier every day. Ben was confined to the little triangle behind the wall, we'd used the counter and the wrecked van to strengthen it and make it higher. Ben, cooped up day and night, grizzled.

A group of people, a deputation they called themselves, set off up the road. They said they were off to Kershaw Farm to confront the soldiers and demand some relief for the town. They didn't return, and a rumour went round that shots had been heard.

Another bunch of survivors walked along the Branford road, intent on plundering a supermarket half a mile outside Skipley. They arrived at dusk to find the place under guard by armed men in fallout-suits. They watched from cover and saw a truck driven out, escorted by two men on motorbikes. The whole outfit headed for the moors.

That's how things were when I set off as usual with my bucket one evening in mid-September. What we'd do was, we'd get a bucketful in the morning to cook and brew tea, and another in the evening for washing. We even washed clothes for a time.

Anyway, I was heading for the Dog and Gun. You had to go up our street, turn left at the top and it was about a quarter of a mile.

Suddenly, someone cried out nearby. The sound seemed to come from a narrow street leading off, and I ran to the end to look.

Coming towards me was a girl. She was running clutching the strap of a plastic sports-bag which swung and bounced against her leg as she ran. Two lads were chasing her, one had a length of heavy chain and the other a whip-aerial off a car.

I'm no hero, and the last thing I wanted right then was a fight. My crotch was still pretty sore, but the lass was only about five yards from me with the two lads close behind. I was dangling the bucket, and as the girl ran past I swung it at the nearest lad. It caught him on the side of the head and he fell. The other one swerved round me and went after the girl. I flung the bucket at his back and set off after him.

The girl was halfway down the street. Her green skirt flew as she ran and the bag bounced against her leg. The lad was gaining on her. As I pelted after them he raised the aerial and swiped her across the shoulder with it. She cried out, swerved and tried to scramble up a mound of smashed bricks. The rubble shifted and she slipped. The lad darted in and seized the bag but the girl held on to the strap. He tugged on the bag and slashed at her repeatedly but she hung on, shielding her head with her free arm.

He was so intent on getting the bag that he didn't look to see where I was till I was nearly on top of him. I snatched up a half-brick and, as he turned, flung it. He clapped both hands to his face. Blood spurted from between his fingers and ran over his hands.

I grabbed the girl by an arm and tried to drag her away.

'No, wait!'

She pulled herself free, bent down and pulled something out of the rubble. It was a bit of iron railing; one of those old ones with a spear tip. The lad I'd clobbered sat curled up, holding his face.

I didn't know what she intended to do until she dropped her bag and lifted the spike above her head with both hands. I stood gaping till it was almost too late then flung myself at her, knocking her sideways and falling on top of her. The rail flew out of her hand and slithered away down the mound. The lad scrambled to his feet and tottered off, holding his face.

I glanced at the long spike, then at the girl. She'd wriggled herself out from underneath me and was knocking dirt off her sleeve. She looked angry. I said, 'You wouldn't have done it, would you, killed him, just like that?'

She glared at me, tight-lipped; straightening her dress. Then her features softened and she said, 'It's going to be us or them, you know.' She picked up the bag and stood dangling it, looking down at me. 'Come on.'

I picked myself up and looked around. Both lads had gone and I said, 'See. You didn't have to be *that* drastic.'

She smiled and I looked at her. She was thin with long, pale hair. Fourteen or so. She had this green dress; thin stripes of white and green really – a school dress, and sandals. Her toes and the tops of her feet were dirty. She seemed nice, which is a crazy thing to say after what she'd meant to do.

Anyway, she said, 'Had a good look, have you?'

I felt my face going red and I said, 'What were they after you for?'

She held up the bag. 'This.'

'What's in it?' I asked. She gave me this incredulous look.

'Food of course. What else?'

Instead of answering I said, 'My name's Danny: what's yours?'

'Kim.'

'Where d'you live?'

She gave a vague wave. 'Over there.'

'Which street?' I persisted.

'Victoria Place,' she said. 'Why?'

I shrugged. 'Just wondered. Will you be all right now?'

She gave a short laugh. 'Sure. Will you?'

'I mean, d'you want me to walk along with you?'

She looked at me coolly. 'Haven't you got your own problems?'

I shrugged again. 'I guess so. But I could see you home if you like.'

'How come you're not after my grub. Or maybe you are?'

'No!' I blurted, angrily. 'I don't need it, we've got a shop.'

As soon as I'd said it I knew I shouldn't have. Dad would have called it drawing attention to our luck. Be thankful for it, he kept saying, but don't draw attention to it.

She must have read the look on my face because she said,

'It's okay. I don't need your stuff either, there's a place I know near Branford.'

'What's it like?' I asked.

'What?'

'Branford.' Talking to her was making me feel real for the first time in days and I didn't want her to go. I said, 'Let's walk towards your place, we can talk as we go.'

She looked at me for a moment without speaking. Then she shrugged and said, 'Okay. But one wrong move and I split, right?'

I nodded. 'Okay.'

We started walking. The sun had dipped below the broken roofs and dusk was seeping through the little streets. 'You want to know what Branford's like?' she said. 'Gone, that's what it's like. One big bomb, one big hole, no Branford.'

'No survivors?'

She shook her head. 'Shouldn't think so. Hole must be fifty feet deep. I've been close four times and I've never seen anybody alive.'

I kicked a lump of brick. 'Two-hundred-thousand people. I wonder who'll tie all the labels on?'

She glanced at me sidelong. 'You don't believe all that stuff, do you?'

'What stuff?'

'What it says in the book.'

I shrugged. 'I was joking about the labels, but somebody'll come eventually.'

She grinned briefly, swinging her bag. 'Who? The enemy? The guys who did this? They're in the same boat we're in, Danny boy.'

'No.' I jerked my head towards the moor. 'Them. The soldiers, or whatever they are. They'll come and sort things out.'

'Why?' There was a mocking light in her eyes.

'Because it's their job,' I snapped. 'That's why. Soldiers always step in where there's a disaster.'

'You're joking!' She swung the bag in a full circle. 'Would *you* come down into this lot if you were sitting up there on the moor in your protective gear on top of a bunkerful of clean grub?' She laughed. 'They're only people you know, like you and me. They want to survive, just like us. You don't think they're about to get all that uncontaminated grub out and start dishing it up to us, do you?'

I shrugged again to hide my unease. The vanished deputation. The shots. What she was saying seemed to be borne out by what had happened up to now.

'I don't know, Kim,' I said. 'It's taking them a long time, but I can't believe they'd just leave us to die.'

'Can't you?' She looked at me sideways. 'I'll tell you something, Mister. If they were down here and I was up there, I'd leave *them* to die, no danger.' She stopped. 'Anyway, this is where I live.'

It was a burnt-out house in a terrace of burnt-out houses. I grinned. 'Better than us,' I said. 'We've only got a cellar.'

'Oh, aye,' she rejoined. 'But it's full of grub though, isn't it?' Her eyes still mocked.

'Look.' I gazed at the cobbles, shuffling my feet. 'I – can we see each other again? Where d'you get your water?'

She grinned. 'Dog and Gun, same as you. Only my sister goes for it.'

'Can you come instead? Tomorrow night?'

She shrugged. 'Dunno. Have to see, won't we? I've got to go in now.'

She turned and walked up the path. There was a charred door. She slapped it with her open hand, twice. It opened. I peered through the gathering twilight, trying to see the sister. There was only a pale blob against the darkness inside. On the step, Kim turned and called softly, 'G'night. Thanks for the rescue act.' Then she was gone, and I said my goodnight to the blackened door.

*   *   *

That night, lying with Ben in the cellar, I couldn't stop thinking about Kim. It was crazy. I mean, I'd known girls I'd liked before, but not so they kept me awake. I lay thinking of things I should have said. I wished I'd been cool or witty or something, instead of stammering. I hadn't even managed to say goodnight before she shut the door for God's sake. The more I went over it in my head, the dafter my performance appeared and the more convinced I became that I'd never see her again. What a twit I'd been, what a pillock.

The fact that she'd been about to kill a bloke was sort of swamped by all these other feelings, and it wasn't hard to find excuses. We were in a new game. The old rules no longer applied. There were no rules in this game; only the ones we made up as we went along. Maybe Kim was better suited to the new game than I was. Maybe I'd had no right to stop her.

I was on guard the last half of the night and I was shattered. I'd hardly slept thinking of Kim and I went on thinking about her as I stood half-frozen, peering into the dark, holding the shotgun Dad had got from somewhere. I kept looking towards Victoria Place, and every time I did I got this ache in my chest. I was like one of those love-lorn prannocks in an old movie.

Anyway, next morning began as usual. Dad came up with the cooker and his shaving tackle. He was the last clean-shaven guy in Skipley. I went for water. I knew Kim wouldn't be there. I kept a lookout for anybody who might be her sister, but the only woman I saw was more like someone's granny. We heated the water and I took Ben's breakfast down to him. He always had this cereal with hot powdered milk. Dad and I ate ours outside and then he shaved sitting hunched forward on his chair, looking into a bit of broken mirror propped up on mine.

Looking back it was a weird time, that first three weeks after the bomb. It was unreal. At least, it felt unreal to me and I suppose it was the same for everybody. One life had ended and the next hadn't begun. We tried to cling to the old life but it slipped away and we drifted in limbo, waiting. That day, the day after I met Kim, was the end of waiting and first day of the new life.

It started after breakfast. We'd washed the bowls and spoons and Ben had stowed them in the cellar. Dad lugged out a big square of canvas and we stood on chairs and draped it over the brickwork so that it made an awning across our little triangle. It sagged in the middle. Dad thought rain might gather there and drag the whole thing down so he pulled some lengths of timber out of the rubble to use like tent-poles. I'd just started digging holes for them when we heard the loudspeaker.

At first it was so far off you couldn't tell which direction it was coming from. I was hitting the ground with the spade when Dad flapped a hand at me. 'Sssh!'

We listened, straining our ears. There was a quacking in the distance like a tin duck and Ben laughed out loud. Dad pressed a finger to his lips and Ben stifled his giggles. The sound came nearer, separating out into warped, unintelligible words.

Somewhere, people started to shout. Dad turned, his eyes shining. 'It's them!' he breathed. 'The soldiers. It must be!' He scooped Ben up in his arms and vaulted with him over the counter. I flung the spade aside and followed. We stood at the roadside, gazing up the street.

Round the corner came a blue car with a loudspeaker on its roof. And after it, whooping and capering in their rags, came a throng of people.

As the procession approached I felt a lump in my throat and my eyes filled with tears. They ran down my cheeks and I didn't care. I remembered a bit of newsreel I saw once; the Allies entering Paris in 1944. People threw flowers. I knew now how they must have felt and I wished I had flowers to throw.

The vehicle was moving at walking speed and as it drew level, it stopped. Its windows were of darkened glass; its occupants dim shapes within. There was a click and the loudspeaker crackled.

'We represent your Local Commissioner,' it said. 'Stand by for a Special Instruction.' There was a brief interval, during which the vehicle's motley escort clapped and cheered. The broadcast continued.

'An emergency hospital has been set up, adjacent to Local Commission Headquarters at Kershaw Farm, and a fleet of ambulances is following this vehicle. Will those of you who are able-bodied please see to it that all burned, sick and badly injured persons are brought out of buildings and placed at the roadside. Please note that only serious cases will be dealt with. Persons suffering from minor injuries will be treated in due course. That is all.'

The car moved on, amid a fresh burst of cheering. I followed it to the bottom of the street then walked back, buoyant with relief. Knots of people were emerging from the ruins, carrying their sick and wounded. Soon the street was lined with them, slumped in arm-chairs or lying on doors and mattresses while relatives hovered near, waiting for the ambulances.

I was amazed how many people there were. Most of them must have remained hidden for the past three weeks in the shells of their houses, because I'd seen very few on the streets or round the well, and the number coming to us for food had hardly altered.

Dad had returned to the job of erecting the poles. I joined him, working happily now that the worst was over. Little Craig Troy appeared and he and Ben played together in the rubble, their shrill voices in our ears as we worked.

It was over an hour before the first ambulance appeared. It wasn't an ambulance, but a canvas-covered military truck with red crosses painted crudely on its sides. It worked its way slowly down the street, stopping every few yards to pick up casualties. As the injured were lifted aboard, relatives clamoured round the tailboard, asking questions in loud, excited voices. When might they visit? How long would this or that patient be gone? What about the dead? All questions were met with shrugs, shaken heads or tinny don't knows.

When the truck was full, the tailboard was slammed shut and the vehicle sped away, scattering spectators. Groans and exclamations followed it from the relatives of those left behind, but shortly afterwards a second truck appeared, and when it eventually rumbled away round the corner, no casualties remained in our street.

People hung about for a while, talking. Dad and I put the finishing touches to our awning, while Ben and his playmate played at soldiers and casualties with a cardboard box for a truck. If they'd known what was happening up at Kershaw Farm, they'd have played at something else.

*   *   *

If the soldiers hadn't come it would have been a long day. I'd have hung around thinking of Kim, worrying myself daft over whether she'd turn up at the well or not. As it was, it was evening before I knew it.

I got the bucket and walked up the street, happier than I'd been since the bomb. Happier than I was before it in a way, because before the bomb I didn't know I was happy.

As I walked, I thought about the people up at the hospital. For three weeks they'd waited in the ruins famished, cold, in pain. We'd heard their cries in the night, but there'd been nothing we could do. Now I pictured them in rows of warm, clean beds; their wounds dressed and their hunger satisfied; drifting to sleep under nurses' watchful eyes. Even those with radiation sickness, who were sure to die, would slip away easily, their minds numbed with sedatives.

And that wasn't all, I told myself. Soon, the less grievously injured would be taken care of; perhaps they'd set up clinics where you'd be able to go, even if you only had toothache or something. And after that there'd be feeding-centres, like it said in the book, with hot meals for all. No need to sit up half the night, guarding the stock.

It made a comfortable picture. I remember I sighed as I imagined it. And the fact that I was on my way to see Kim was the icing on my cake.

She hadn't arrived when I got there. There were two guys in the cobbled yard. I loitered by the archway that led into the yard.

I was just beginning to worry when I turned, and she was there. Same dress, dangling a bucket. Something turned over in my chest and my face burned.

'Oh, hi Kim,' I said lightly. This time I'd be cool.

'Hello,' she said. 'Been waiting long?'

'Just got here. Thought you'd been and gone.' Cool.

She shrugged. 'What were you hanging about for, then?'

'Waiting for them.' I nodded towards the two men. They were coming through the arch with their water.

We went through into the yard. I stood watching as she lowered the bucket. There was this bucket that was there all the time. It was on a rope. You hauled the water up in that and tipped it into your own. When she had the bucket full I took hold of the rope. She didn't let go and we pulled together, our hands and hips touching. The rope could have been two miles long and the bucket would still have come up too soon for me.

My run of luck wasn't over, either, because when I started to haul my own water up she took hold and pulled with me. Hand and hip. Cool on the surface, hot inside.

'Think I'll walk back your way,' I said, casually.

She smiled. 'Miles out of your way,' she mocked. 'Nobody waiting for the water?'

'Dad,' I said. 'He can wait.' I went to pick up both buckets. She grabbed hers and pulled it away, slopping a little.

'I can manage,' she said. 'I'm not paralysed, you know.'

I shrugged. 'Being a gentleman, that's all.'

'Haven't you heard,' she said. 'Gentlemen are out. Cavemen rule, okay?'

We left the yard.

Her crack about cavemen had reminded me of the soldiers. I said, 'You were wrong about the soldiers: they did come.' I looked sideways at her. The water was heavy and she walked tilted over to the right. She frowned.

'They came,' she said. 'But don't you think it was a bit funny?'

'What, taking the casualties away? What's funny about it?'

'There's this old couple,' she said. 'Next door but one. The old woman's burned all down one side. We took her out this morning, and they loaded her in with a lot of others. The old guy was upset. Maureen, that's my sister, asked when he could go up and visit his wife. The soldiers just shook their heads. Didn't say any time, or that visiting isn't allowed or anything. And when she asked again they sort of pushed her aside and moved off. It didn't seem right to me.'

'They'll be fantastically busy,' I said. 'There must be thousands of casualties. There'll be no time for frills like visiting.'

'That's another thing.' She kicked a stone and watched it skip along the flags. 'How the heck do they intend to look after thousands of people? What sort of hospital can you build in three weeks? I think they had something to hide, and that's why they wouldn't answer Maureen.'

'Rubbish!' I hadn't meant to talk to her like that, but she seemed intent on messing up what till now had been a perfect day. I was about to tell her so when a commotion broke out behind us. We turned.

A man was coming along the street. A cripple. He dragged one leg and hung onto things, moving in a series of jerky swoops from one support to the next; shouting in this high, cracked voice. He was too far off for us to make out what he was saying.

As we watched, a couple of men came out and grabbed him and sat him down on the bonnet of a burnt-out car. He went on shouting, waving his arms about and trying to get up. One of the men called out and a woman came running. The man said something to her and she sank down on the pavement with her hands over her ears, shaking her head.

'Something's happened!' cried Kim. 'Come on.' She put down the bucket and began running back towards the group round the car.

I stood gazing after her while dread spread like cold water across my guts. I couldn't move. I remember thinking: Perhaps if I stand very still it'll be all right. It'll be all right.

I didn't even put the bucket down. She looked back when she reached the car but she was too far away for me to see the expression on her face.

She was talking to them. The men on the bonnet had quietened down but the woman still sat doubled up on the ground. Kim bent and touched her hands but she didn't respond. Kim started walking towards me, slowly, till I could see her eyes. They weren't looking at me. They weren't looking at anything. When she came up to me she didn't speak, but lifted the bucket and walked on. I transferred mine to the other hand and hurried after her.

When we came to her gateway, she turned in without speaking and I called after her, 'Kim?' The cake had crumbled into dust and the icing was melting.

She stopped and turned. When she spoke her voice was dead, like her eyes.

'They shot them, Danny,' she said. 'Every one of them. People heard shots and ran up the road. They saw an earthmover and some pits. Guys in fallout-suits opened fire on them. That man back there got clear.' She paused, biting her lip and gazing at the ground. 'That won't be the end of it,' she continued in the same, flat voice. 'Now that they've killed off the sick, they'll be after somebody else – old people maybe, or kids. And after that, somebody else and somebody else, till it comes down to us. Us or them.' She looked me up and down, assessing my chances. 'Cavemen versus gentlemen is no contest,' she said. 'We've got to be as hard as they are, Danny boy – or harder. See you.'

I stood watching till the door closed, then made my way homeward in the dusk. Fires flickered in some of the houses. Cooking smells hung on the air and I caught fragments of conversation. Somebody played a mouth-organ, and a loud guffaw burst out from the darkness beyond a frameless window.

I pictured them, these invisible people, happy as I had been, imagining their loved ones safe and warm. Knowing the reality, the sick, going to their deaths with our cheering in their ears, I attempted indifference. Compassion belonged to the old life. Hardness was the thing.

So they're dead, I hissed. So what?

Then I thought about this old man, waiting for his wife to come home, and how she was beautiful to him, even though she was just an ugly old woman. He'd wait and wait and never see her again, even though he'd wait for ever if he could. And I started to cry, and trailed along humping the bucket while tears ran down my face. Cavemen versus gentlemen. Hardness versus compassion. No contest.

The Child

Smell fresh water while you can,
While still a creature free from man.
His influence doesn't reach you yet,
He regards you as an insignificant pet.
You're too ignorant to understand
The filth and plotting man has planned.

But that's a blessing; saved a bit from something sinister,
Though it means you're ill-prepared to meet with man –
  the monster.

Your thoughts are simple and straightforward,
So what if they say it's untoward?
But alas, you *do* have a narrow view,
Not enough scope to realise what they'll do to you.

For, contaminated you have been born,
There's but one restricted way for you to form;
You must, one day, become all they are,
Yes, those things you watch being wicked from afar.

The gradual change will happen every day,
You'll feel your attitudes start to sway.
You'll feel it happen, but you'll be helpless, you know,
Your old emotions are things you'll be frightened to show.

For every innocent freedom is a preventative law,
They point at you, saying – immature!

When your programming's over, and by their ugly standards
  you're near correct,
They throw you in alone among their sect.
No matter that you try to fight the change away,
You'll wake up and belong with them one day.

So, stay on the beach. Go on playing with your sand.
You don't appreciate the anguish that's at hand.
Take advantage while you can still be wild,
Before they change your happy state; a child.

David Upshall

Free As I Know

I am black as I thought
My lids are as brown as
I thought
My hair is curled as I
thought
I am free as I know.

Accabre Huntley

Follow On

The activities suggested in this section are intended to help you enjoy and explore the various texts through developing
– your perception of different characters
– your understanding of the author's perspective
– your awareness of the author's use of language
– your own responses and views
– your own use of language.

Many of the activities should assist you in building up a folder for the coursework element of the General Certificate of Secondary Education. There are opportunities for imaginative, personal, critical and discursive writing. Apart from suggestions related to each main text, there are also topics for extended studies. These involve exploring
– a theme occurring in a number of different pieces
– the work of a particular author
– a particular mode of writing.

Talking about your ideas is often recommended before putting pen to paper. Listening to other people's responses and views can be an excellent stimulus to clarifying your own. I have also suggested that when you feel you need further information, you write to appropriate organisations. It is also fun as well as instructive to imagine using different media for communication, e.g. radio, television, theatre. You may well think of possibilities for exploring these media other than those already suggested. There is a mixture of individual, group and whole class work but perhaps you will want to make adaptations at times in order to develop areas of special interest.

As said in the introduction, I hope this collection will arouse you to respond strongly, with both heart and mind. Literature lives through our responses to it. While the focus within the texts is on young people being challenged by their experiences to consider themselves and their society, I hope that your imaginations will also be challenged...and that you will enjoy extending your personal language in expressing your own perceptions and reflections on the world that we all share.

an extract from
'Tell Freedom'

THE AUTHOR'S description of the physical environment plays an important part in our own understanding of the conditions under which the community is living. Note the way the writer builds up these details.

Write a short story set in your local environment in which physical conditions play a prominent part.

LEE IS involved in two arguments in this extract–one with Andries and the other with the white boys. In a small group discuss the essential differences in these arguments.

You will need to consider the question of name-calling and different levels or kinds of name-calling. Discuss Lee's responses as well as your own, both to his situation and your own experiences of name-calling. Do you accept the saying 'Sticks and stones may break my bones but words will never hurt me'?

You might find it helpful to consider what was written by the young playwright Hanif Kureishi, author of the film My Beautiful Launderette. Born in London, with an English mother and a father from Pakistan, he heard frequent talk about the 'pakis', one teacher even calling him 'Pakistani Pete':

> *I was desperately embarrassed and afraid of being identified with these loathed aliens. I found it almost impossible to answer questions about where I came from. The word 'pakistani' had been made into an insult. It was a word I didn't want used about myself. I couldn't tolerate being myself... I suspected that my white friends were capable of racial insults. And many of them did taunt me innocently. I reckoned that at least every day since I was five years old, I had been racially abused. I became incapable of distinguishing between remarks that were genuinely intended to hurt me and those intended as 'humour'.*

> Reprinted by permission of Faber and Faber Limited from
> *My Beautiful Launderette The Rainbow Sign* by Hanif Kureishi.

After your discussion, prepare a talk on the subject. Include what you think should be done about it.

IN THIS passage Lee undergoes two 'breaking-ins' by adults to living under white domination. In a small group, discuss the role of Andries in the first and Uncle Sam in the second. Why are Aunt Liza's reactions so important to Lee? What do you think her response would have been to the white farmer if Uncle Sam hadn't been there and she had been expected to 'teach' her nephew?

AFTER CONSIDERING carefully Aunt Liza's qualities,

imagine you are researching material for a radio programme on the author Peter Abrahams. From his autobiography *Tell Freedom* you gather that Aunt Liza made a deep impression on him and you want to understand her more fully. Prepare your questions and write up what might be her answers. Bear in mind that as an interviewer you have to help her feel at ease.

You might first try actually interviewing elderly people about their working lives and bringing up children. If you tape these interviews and listen to them, you should be able to identify elements which encourage a free flow of conversation and reminiscence. Try to incorporate these elements into your imagined interview so that it is not stilted.

WHY DOES the white farmer use Uncle Sam to enforce his control? Discuss in a small group Uncle Sam's feelings. Imagine that he too is interviewed and write up the questions and answers.

THIS COULD be seen as a very depressing extract. Discuss in a small group whether you see it simply as depressing or whether you feel anything positive in it.

Lee is physically beaten down. To what extent is he mentally crushed? If you think he isn't totally broken, discuss why you think this. What importance do you place on learning something through an experience, even if it is very unpleasant? The white farmer intends Lee to be taught a lesson. What do you think he learnt?

*An extract from
'I Know Why The Caged
Bird Sings'*

BEFORE READING, consider the title.

STOP READING after the words 'Mrs. Randall's maid was talking as she took the soup from me, and I wondered what her name used to be and what she answered to now.' (page 23) In pairs, predict how Marguerite tackled the problem. What would you have wanted to do in that situation and what might you have done?

IN DESCRIBING Mr. Cullinan, the author writes 'Her husband remains, in my memory, undefined. I lumped him with all the other white men that I had ever seen and tried not to see.' In a small group discuss why you think she has this reaction.

THE CENTRAL experience – of being called 'out of one's name' – is deeply humiliating and painful, yet this extract is also entertaining and refreshing. This seems due to Maya Angelou's spirited narration and the ways in which she sees through the pretensions of Mrs. Cullinan. In pairs look for examples. Then write an assessment of Maya Angelou's style and what it communicates about her as a person. Use quotations from the text. You may also refer to her poem 'Still I Rise'.

IN PAIRS discuss why you think Miss Glory defends Mrs. Cullinan so stoutly. Consider her history. Imagine her telling a friend about Marguerite and the central incident and write up the conversation. Before writing, try role-playing the two parts with a partner.

EITHER REWRITE this extract as a play. Note stage directions, including details of location and characterisation.
OR REWRITE the events in the form of a poem. You can use or adapt phrases and sentences from the story, as well as using your own words or ideas. Try to let it convey Maya Angelou's spirit.

THE NARRATION covers a few weeks. Using details and information you have picked up from your reading, write one of the scenes in more detail. You could perhaps focus on one of her conversations with Bailey, or with Miss Glory. Write in the third person.

AT THE age of ten Maya Angelou was already doing a full day's work. There are still countries where young children are doing adult work. Find out what you can about present day child workers. The Anti-Slavery Society has produced reports on child workers in various countries, including places like South Africa, India, Spain, Italy etc. (Anti-Slavery Society, 180 Brixton Road, London SW9 6AT). You could contact them or other organisations concerned with children, e.g. CAFOD Development Education Department, (2 Garden Close, Stockwell Road, London SW9 9TY). Are there situations in which you think children who work are not being exploited but are taking on an adult role because of the way their culture is organised? When you have completed your research, prepare a talk on your findings and your own views.

An extract from
'Basketball Game'

BEFORE READING, in a small group discuss situations in which you have either ignored parental advice or have gone against a parent's instructions. Have any of these situations involved forbidden friendships? In retrospect do you think you were right to act as you did?

DURING READING, stop at the break in the text, after 'Rev. Anderson probably thought he was still upset by their argument at dinner the other day. At least Allen hoped that's what he thought. His mother probably knew it had something to do with Rebecca, though she didn't know he was going out with her Monday.' (page 35) The argument had been about Rebecca after his father had seen him with her. Allen had insisted it wasn't a crime for him to talk to her, while his father had warned him fiercely to stay away from her...

> 'I'm just trying to tell you something for your own good. You the only son I got and I don't want to see you hanging from the end of a rope. You don't know these white folks. You been up North all your life. But these peckerwoods down here are crazy. You hear me, boy? They crazy! I grew up with a boy named Willie Johnson and they hanged Willie 'cause he didn't say "ma'am" to a white woman.'

Another black man known to Allen's father had been lynched because of a white girlfriend. When the couple had been discovered she had turned on him, accusing him of rape.

In pairs discuss what you feel Allen should do about Rebecca's invitation to accompany him to Peabody College.

> He wanted to do the same thing to her, but for some reason he couldn't.

WHY DOES Allen let Rebecca take unfair advantage of him in each basketball game? Discuss this in a small group or in pairs. To appreciate the strength of his conflict, refer to your own feelings in a situation where someone has taken advantage of you.

IMAGINE ALLEN keeps a diary. In pairs, discuss the sorts of things he might record, then write up the entries for the following days:
– the first Saturday he plays basketball with Rebecca
– the Thursday he shows her his paintings
– the Monday they go to Peabody College.
Let the diary reveal why he continues with his visit to Peabody College despite his fear. Decide what you think it is that drives Allen on. Consider the tone in which the diary would be written. You

could incorporate words from the passage if this is appropriate.

Still, Allen was pleased that his father had defended him. He could've acted like he had with the man in the filling station.

ALLEN IS surprised that his father has stood up to Rebecca's father. In a small group discuss what you think might have happened at the filling station.

IN A small group discuss the possibilities for the scenes omitted from this extract: of Allen and Rebecca going to Peabody College, and of the following confrontation between the two fathers. You could act out the two scenes and/or write them as a story, or a script for a play or film.

If you want to base the college scene on ideas from the book, read the following excerpts and consider the accompanying questions:

Allen tried to eradicate them from his mind, like he usually did when he was around white people. He wondered if Rebecca noticed the people. She didn't seem to.

Who and what is Allen trying to eradicate?

She would talk about all the things she wanted to do or did do, and all of them would be things he couldn't do. So he didn't want to hear her.

What is the source of Allen's irritation?

'If my daddy could see your paintings and know how smart you are, I bet he would like you. I bet if he really knew you were different than other colored people, it would be all right.'

How would you feel if you were Allen?

'Do you know that colored man?' she asked, pointing to an old man in work clothes who was beckoning to Allen from the edge of the grass. Allen didn't know anyone in Nashville and wondered what the man wanted with him. Had somebody seen them and was going to call the police?

What do you think the old man wanted to say to Allen?

When you are discussing the confrontation between the two fathers, consider the professions of both men and why you think Allen's father stands his ground.

*P*rivate Eloy

DURING READING, stop after the wounded young rebel says to Eloy 'Come with us...You carry me and I'll guide you.' In pairs discuss what you think Eloy should do.

IF YOU think Eloy should have made a different decision from that in the story, rewrite the ending.

LIST ELOY'S reasons for joining and remaining in the army. Quote from the text to illustrate his feelings about the positive aspects of army life for him. Then list all the reasons for leaving. Again use quotations to show how he is emotionally affected by his experiences.

Despotism was reaping its natural harvest and now the soldiers were going out to fight the rebels in the mountains.

THIS STORY is based on an actual period in Cuba's history when guerilla bands were formed in the mountains after a couple of unsuccessful attacks and attempts at uprisings against the dictator Batista. Find out what you can about the revolution in Cuba. (Consult the further reading list or the anthology from which this story is drawn.)

Then prepare two speeches, one from the politician who obtained a place for Eloy in the army and the other from one of the rebel leaders. The speeches are to be given after Eloy's death in his parents' village. The politician comes to the village during the day on an army recruitment drive. (With the growing success of the guerillas it is now necessary to persuade young men to enlist.) The guerilla leader comes to the village secretly at night.

You could also act out the meetings and include Eloy's family amongst the villagers.

IMAGINE YOU are a journalist wanting to investigate the dual hangings. Whom would you interview? Make notes for your article before writing it. You will need to include some background material on the social conflict and also describe the setting. Working in a group, you could also tape-record the interviews and use these as a basis for writing up your report for publication.

Small Avalanches

BEFORE READING talk about the title in pairs. After reading, discuss it again and decide why the author chose it.

WHAT MIGHT happen to Nancy that evening when her uncle discovers the car of the man from Kansas still parked by the side of the road. Imagine the man is found semi-conscious, mumbling something about Nancy leaving him there. In a small group discuss and then act this out.

STORIES CAN carry underlying messages. Which of the following might apply to this one?
Don't walk home alone on lonely paths.
Men shouldn't smile at young girls.
Don't go with strangers under any circumstances.
People who aren't fit shouldn't run up hills.
When you feel uneasy about an adult's behaviour, don't delay in finding and confiding in another adult you can trust.
Talk about these alternatives in a small group. What do you think Nancy should have done? Write up your views in an essay. Do you think stories like this should be included in collections for a young readership?

NANCY CLOSELY escapes a dangerous situation. How aware do you think she is that she might have been attacked? Look closely at her responses and try to explain them. If her cousin Georgia suggested they try hitching a lift again, would she refuse? Discuss these questions in pairs and write up a possible conversation between the two cousins.

IN A small group talk about what you would do if you were the teachers in Nancy's school. Do you think more needs to be done in your school on this issue? If so, write up your suggestions. If you are concerned that there is not enough focus on the issue, discuss it further with your teacher. You could write a group letter to your education authority asking what is being done to educate children about abuse and how to handle it.

IN PAIRS look through the story to see how the author uses physical details to indicate Nancy's state of mind and also the man's. Then discuss the story's structure–the way it begins and ends at home. What is your response to the ending, with Nancy being thrown her brother's shirt for ironing? Why do you think the author chose to end it this way?

Using the same attention to detail and perhaps a similar structure, write a story which involves potential danger. Decide whether you will write in the first or third person.

an extract from
'Hand On The Sun'

AT THE beginning of a novel an author may use a quotation which sums up an important aspect of the novel as a whole. In *Hand On The Sun* there is the following inscription:

> 'To hold a people down forever is like putting a hand on the sun.' – El Salvadorian graffiti.

Before reading, discuss the title and this inscription.

IMAGINE JALIB receives a letter from one of his friends in Pakistan saying he also hopes to come to England. Write Jalib's reply. He could tell his friend about particular incidents to illustrate what has been happening to him. Let him be frank about the conflicts he has experienced. You could discuss these in a small group before writing. You might wish to consider the following:
– his original ideas about England and the reality for him
– the ordeal of passing through the immigration officers
– his father's ambitions for him and his chances of achieving them
– the lives his parents are leading.

IN A small group research and discuss how stories about immigrants are often reported in newspapers. Such reports are usually written from a perspective 'outside' the immigrant community. If possible, look at reporting of the same events in different newspapers. It would be especially useful to look at press like the Caribbean Times, Asian Times, African Times, West Indian World, The Daily Jang.

IMAGINE JALIB and his friends form a Youth Organisation when they are a few years older. They are given the chance to make a programme for community television about their lives. Write the outline of the proposal they have to submit to the series editor in

the television company. You will need to consider:
– what form the programme will take
– what issues are to be highlighted
– who is to be interviewed
– what scenes are to be depicted.

JALIB'S MOTHER and father have different opinions about how their son should be treated. Write about these differences in the form of a play. Consider his father's attitude to putting up with harrassment. Imagine his mother suggests they should return to Pakistan as soon as possible because she thinks that Jalib will also end up working seven days a week in a factory or mill.

You will need to think about his mother's life in England. What was it like for her to move from a community and village she knew to a strange country where she feels unwelcome? Before you begin writing your dialogue practise role-playing in pairs so that it sounds as realistic as possible.

He knew that the goras were in India for a long time, but not why. He had often wondered if the goras were treated, in India, the same way he and his family were treated here.

RESEARCH AND discuss these questions that puzzle Jalib. When consulting books and other material about the British in India, try to make out the perspectives of the authors. Write a report of your discussion.

IMAGINE JALIB ten years older, working in the same mill as his father. The younger workers are dissatisfied with pay and conditions. Discuss in a small group and write up the following:
– a short report on the situation by the factory manager
– a speech by Jalib at a meeting of workers in which he refers back to his childhood experiences
– editorials for two newspapers with opposing political views.
Predict an outcome for the situation and write Jalib's comments in response to a television news reporter.

When completed this could be turned into a dramatic presentation.

...the education he received wouldn't come in the classroom but in the playground.

WRITE AN essay or prepare a talk on this theme. Although you should begin with Jalib's experience, you need not restrict yourself to the extract. You might want to consider your own playground education and your response to Adrian Mitchell's poem 'Back In The Playground Blues'.

a personal essay,
'Young, Gifted And Black'

THE UPPER school, set in the leafy suburb away from the factories, had previously been the old grammar school. Although its building isn't described, how do you imagine it to be? In pairs, discuss the school buildings within your own area. If you have examples of old grammar and secondary modern buildings, find out when they were built and discuss whether there are basic differences. Consider the front doors, the flooring (if you can go inside), the grounds etc. Do you think any of the differences are (or were) important? Do they tell you anything about our society? Does the type of school building you are in affect you? Do you think it affects your teachers? You could interview and tape different people on the subject before preparing a talk. Illustrate your talk with examples from the interviews.

MANY SECONDARY schools have now done away with separate 'remedial' classes and offer their students support in other ways. What is the position in your school? Find out the arguments used for and against separate classes. After interviewing a range of teachers, children and parents, prepare an essay in which you quote various viewpoints. Come to your own conclusions.

IN A small group consider the sort of events which might have led up to one of the singers being sent away to a school for 'maladjusted' children. Who would have made the decision? Imagine the scene when the head of lower school informed the girl's mother and father about the decision. It is possible that her behaviour at home was different from that at school. Think of her parents' hopes and expectations, the hardships they experienced in setting up a home for their children in England, the little time they had to spend with their daughter, etc. Act it out.

IMAGINE AN interview ten years later with the young woman who was that girl called 'maladjusted', and write it up. Let her reflect on:
– her childhood in the Caribbean and in England
– her grandparents who had to be left behind, and her parents with whom she came to live after being separated for a few years
– her schooling
– her responses to racism and her feelings about the society.

OTHER PHRASES from this essay could have been chosen for the title. Read it through again in pairs and select other alternatives. On what does 'To Be Young, Gifted And Black' place the main focus? Would you have selected this title or another one? Explain your choice.

IN 1985 the government published a report called 'Education for All: the report of the Committee of Inquiry into the Education of Children from Ethnic Minority Groups'. It said that Britain is a multicultural society and that pupils should be helped to understand what this means. It also urged that *all* schools should adopt clear policies to combat racism and that it was especially necessary for schools in 'all-white' areas to recognise that they needed to tackle racist ideas and practices. (A summary of the Swann report is available from The Runnymede Trust, 37a Grays Inn Road, London WC1X 8PP.)

Find out the position in your school about a policy against racism. You might need to interview some senior members of staff. You could also write to the Director of Education to find out what the local education authority has done to develop such policies in all schools in the area. What are the issues you think need to be tackled? If your school already has a policy, how well does it work?

When you have completed your research and discussions, draw up your own report on combatting racism which you might give to appropriate people. For this project you could carry out initial discussions in small groups, coming together to share and collaborate at each stage as a class.

India

WHILE YOU are reading pay particular attention to the story's style and structure. For example,
– to whom is it addressed?
– how would you sum up this style of writing?
– how do you respond to it?
– if the story had been written chronologically, where would the opening section fit in?

LOOK CLOSELY at the way different characters are presented and how the author brings them alive. After discussion in pairs write up an incident in which you try to use the same techniques of crisp, lively characterisation.

WRITE THE scene in which Inderjit confronts Goldfinger about his engagement.

THE NARRATIVE style and structure of 'India' is unusual:
– it is written colloquially, as if the narrator is addressing the reader directly–there are even breaks in the text for direct questions.
– it could be said that this story begins somewhere in the middle and ends with the introduction of a new character and situation.
In pairs, discuss the narrative style and structure; why the writer might have chosen to present it in this way and whether she is successful.

DISCUSS IN a small group, what you understand by the word 'cynical'. What is the difference between 'cynical' and 'sceptical'? Are there ideas or things about which you are either cynical or sceptical? Are there other things about which you are optimistic? Is there anything about which you are really pessimistic? Develop a play around an issue in which different characters express and argue from these different perspectives.

THE ISSUE of arranged marriages forms part of this story but so-called 'free' marriages also come in for criticism.
   In pairs or small groups consider the marriage and courtship traditions *you* have been brought up to expect within your family:
– how far do they help ensure the compatability and happiness of the couple themselves?
– how far do they place importance on outward appearances?
– are there differences in expectation for boys and girls?
– are there other expectations and pressures from your peers?
You could also discuss the attitude of Inderjit's mum: 'you've got to work for everything in life, things don't come from out of nowhere on a silver thali'. (A 'thali' is a necklace given by a bridegroom to a bride on marriage, like a wedding ring.)

THIS STORY was first published in a collection of short stories by women writers called *More To Life Than Mr Right*.
   Write an essay in which you assess the reasons why 'India' is an appropriate story for a collection with this title.
   Before you start planning your essay consider the following questions:
– which is the most rewarding relationship in the story?
– what are the different expectations placed on Inderjit–from her family and people at school, including Goldfinger?
– why does she feel relaxed with Goldfinger?
– what makes her so cynical by the end of the story?

*T*rue Grit, Hard Graft

Often while I was reading in bed at night I would hear the more private conversation between my mum and dad.

ARE THERE issues from which you think your parents try to protect you? Talk about this in pairs. Then act and/or write out a scene where you decide to bring one of these issues into the open.

DAWN NEWTON observes in some detail what happened to members of her family during a period of great stress. Working in pairs, make a list of all the changes she records in herself as well as in other members of the family. Discuss these and then think about a period of change or tension for your own family. (It need not be so great as that in Dawn's family.) Describe in writing as accurately as possible the changes in behaviour you observed, including your own.

IN A small group discuss what brought about the author's concern with politics. What is your own level of interest, and can you explain your interest or lack of it? If you were to meet Dawn Newton what sort of conversation might you have with her? Choose one person in the group to be Dawn and try it out. You can discuss a range of different topics with her. Afterwards tape and/or write up either your conversation with her, or an imagined interview for a local radio station.

DURING THE strike the author was upset by remarks made at school by people who didn't want to understand the position of her family. Write a poem about her being put down in this way.

THE AUTHOR says that she used to be selfish and the experience of the strike helped her understand other people in difficulty. Do you think it is always necessary to experience some form of hardship yourself before you can understand the hardship of others? Write an essay on this.

THE AUTHOR writes that she would watch television eagerly, even if only to 'jeer and contradict'. Imagine that she and some friends want to make a programme which would allow the perspective of young people like themselves to be seen. Put yourselves in their position and in a small group, discuss what should be the important features of the film. It would be helpful to read other pieces from the anthology *More Valuable Than Gold* and have more information on the strike.

Prepare an outline of ideas to submit to the television company. You will need to indicate what is to be screened and who is to be interviewed, remembering that the focus is on young people. You may decide to use selected poems from the anthology to provide the central themes.

Afterwards, imagine that a producer at the television company says she is interested in your outline, but is worried that you have omitted to give a voice to the children of those miners who ignored the strike by continuing to work. She says she realises there is a great bitterness about 'scabbing', but will only make the film if you incorporate the views of these children too. Discuss your responses:

– will you change your film, and if so how? What effect would the changes have? Write a new outline.

– if you feel it is impossible to change the film without altering what you want to say, write a letter to the producer expressing your position. Give your reasons.

Homecoming

THE EARLIEST journey which the author recollects was made just before the 'Soweto Uprising'. Find out about and discuss the events to which she is referring. (You could consult the book on young people's resistance in South Africa called *The Child Is Not Dead* – see Further Reading.)

WHY DO you think the author's parents felt their children were in need of a 'reorientation programme' even though it meant them going into the land of apartheid?

WHAT IMPORTANCE do you place on being part of a family which extends beyond parents and children? Do you see grandparents, aunts, uncles, and cousins only from time to time or do you all work as a close unit, helping each other out? Western families are often said to be based on 'nuclear', i.e. mother/father/children, rather than 'extended' units. In a small group discuss what this means. What circumstances can lead 'extended families' to become 'nuclear' families?

THE AUTHOR comments 'You and I know about home being where the heart is and about home being sweet, but do you know of a deep intense feeling of belonging?'

Have you felt that deep sense of attachment to a place? What is it that gives you that feeling? You could try expressing your thoughts in a poem.

IN A small group or in pairs, discuss the author's reactions to living in Wales and England. Looking back on her period in Sheffield, she says 'I managed to become part of it all, although when I look back, I realise that most of it was pretence.'

Can you think of situations where you have pretended to yourself that you are at ease and part of everything? Discuss why people do this and what enables them to give up pretending. Imagine you write a monthly advice column in a magazine for young people. Write a piece on this theme.

THE AUTHOR must have known something about apartheid, even when she was twelve. Yet her shock is genuine. How do you explain this? If you can recall an event which shocked you–but also gave you a wider awareness–write about your experience.

HOW WOULD you describe the author's tone throughout most of this story? Why is the ending so effective? You could try using the same device yourself either in the task suggested above or in a short story.

If Someone Were To Ask Me...

GLOSSARY

Robben Island: a top-security island prison for political prisoners, 10 km off the coast of Cape Town.

Crossroads: A black squatter camp outside the 'white' city of Cape Town which, after continual police attempts to destroy it, became a symbol of defiance against apartheid. Most of its inhabitants were escaping from the even more desperate poverty of the 'homelands' where there is no work, but to which the authorities kept trying to move them. Many women, with children, were also asserting their right to live alongside their husbands, despite not having permission in their 'pass' documents. In 1986, after eleven years of resistance, the homes of more than 30,000 people in Crossroads were finally razed to the ground by the fire, sticks and knives of the government-supported vigilantes known as 'witdoeke' – men with white head scarves.

KTC: another squatter camp near Crossroads, also destroyed by vigilantes in 1986.

'Homelands': 13% of South Africa is set aside for occupation by Africans, who form 75% of the population. Africans are assigned to a 'homeland' on the basis of language and can be forcibly removed there even though they may never have been to the 'homeland' before.

Transkei: the area which the South African authorities have set up as a 'homeland' for Xhosa speakers. Once fertile, the land has deteriorated through enforced over-population. The authorities refer to it now as an 'independent republic', as if it and its people are no longer part of South Africa. The reference in the poem 'South Africa' to black miners who 'are only/employed for eleven months a year/so they don't become citizens' relates to the complicated laws controlling Africans' rights to reside in 'white' areas, and to the process of removing South African citizenship from Africans.

Soweto: to the south-west of Johannesburg, this is a vast complex of mainly monotonous, grey 'matchbox' houses, spread over 32 square miles, accommodating the one and a half million black workers of the 'white' city.

IN PAIRS discuss the following questions:

'Grandad':
  For what sort of reason might the author's grandfather have been imprisoned? What sentence do you think he received?

What makes this poem so powerful? Look closely at the development of images and the author's responses.

'Shanty Town':
How does the author bring Crossroads alive? Note again the progression of images and emotions.
What is the final effect of the poem on you?

'South Africa':
Have you come across tourist images of South Africa and does it bother you that glossy pictures can cover up another reality?
What does Nzwaki's action say to you?

EACH OF these poems contains a strong central contrast with which the author himself is grappling. In pairs, look at each poem again and say what you think that contrast is.
Use the ideas from this discussion and those which occurred to you during reading to write an appreciation of the poems.

LOOKING AT the three poems together, discuss the effect of the refrain 'If someone were to ask me what it's like... I would tell that person...'.
Use this refrain to write a poem of your own on a subject about which you feel strongly.

*T*ell Freedom
*H*omecoming
*I*f Someone Were To Ask Me...

MANY YOUNG black South Africans today say they are not prepared to put up with what their parents have suffered and are prepared if necessary to die in the struggle to create a democratic society. Write a poem on your own responses to apartheid. Your responses may be based on particular incidents in these pieces and/or on other knowledge you have about South Africa (through television, newspapers, wider reading, etc).

YOU WANT to make a television documentary about South Africa called 'If Someone Were To Ask Me What It's Like...'. In order to do this you have to write an outline of the programme to submit to the television company. In your outline you should give details of the visual material to be shown, people to be interviewed etc. You might also want to have extracts from the three poems read as a 'voice-over' to accompany some of the film. With research, this could be developed into an extended assignment, in which, for instance, you write up imagined interviews with a variety of South Africans; include an excerpt from an imagined play being shown secretly to a Soweto audience etc. You might also want to include some historical background to show the origins of apartheid and the long history of resistance to it. The further reading list will be useful to you.

THE UNITED Nations Organisation has called apartheid 'a crime against humanity' which should concern the whole world. Write an essay in which you respond not only to the material presented here on South Africa, but in which you consider the description 'a crime against humanity'. Consult the list of further reading.

EXAMINE NEWSPAPER coverage of South Africa. Look across a range of newspapers (available in a public library) and if possible on a number of days. It is usually possible to photocopy material in a public library. It would be useful for you to compare this coverage with the weekly selection of items drawn mainly from the South African press by the African National Congress. (Ask for a copy of 'News Briefing' from the ANC, Box 38, 28 Penton Street, London N1 9PR. Specify the week in which you are interested.) Bear in mind that there is strict censorship of all news in South Africa.

Look closely in the British newspapers for differences
– in how much space is allocated
– in what events are selected
– in the way people and events are described, e.g. the language used
– in the people or sources quoted
– in the amount of background material given to help the reader.

Once you have collected your material and conducted any other research necessary, write a critical assessment of the newspaper coverage.

You could extend this project by interviewing people on what they know and think about apartheid. Find out what newspapers they read and consider whether this is significant.

A further extension of the assignment would be to watch television coverage, asking the same questions as those for newspapers. Consider whether the coverage of particular events would have been different if the author of 'If Someone Were To Ask Me...' had been the reporter.

an extract from '*Brother In The Land*'

BEFORE READING, try to get a copy of the booklet, *Protect And Survive* (HMSO 1980). Discuss in small groups the instructions and advice it gives on surviving a nuclear attack in the light of what you would imagine to be the conditions.

DURING READING note the build-up of references to Kershaw Farm. In pairs, discuss your responses at each of the following places:

Stop reading after the words 'a rumour went round that shots had been heard' (page 110). What is at Kershaw Farm and why might there be rumours?

Stop reading after Danny says ' "I can't believe they'd just leave us to die." ' (page 114) Do you find yourself holding out hope, like Danny?

Stop reading after the arrival of the car with the loudspeaker and the words 'The car moved on, amid a fresh burst of cheering.' Predict what happens.

AFTER READING in a small group discuss your initial opinions and whether you would now revise any of them or have any new thoughts to add.

THE AUTHOR writes in the first person, in a very direct, almost casually straight-forward style. Why do you think he chose to write in this way? Write an essay noting examples which you think particularly effective, giving your reasons. Consider, for example, the effect of Danny's statement: 'I'm no hero, and the last thing I wanted right then was a fight.' (page 111); and his thoughts on Kim: 'It was crazy. I mean, I'd known girls I'd liked before, but not so they kept me awake.' (page 114)

WRITE ABOUT the initial differences in outlook between Danny and Kim, giving examples. Describe how Danny finds himself being forced to change. Do you feel yourself to be more like Danny or like Kim in your own responses?

DANNY SEEMS to have read *Protect And Survive*. It includes this advice:

> Listen to your radio for information about the services and facilities as they become available and about the type of cases which are to be treated as urgent.

If possible read the book for yourself. Find out what is the position in your area by contacting your local authority (Civil Defence officer) and Campaign for Nuclear Disarmament group. Working in pairs, prepare a joint talk on your findings and on your own views on the situation.

IMAGINE KIM also decides to keep a record of her experience of living 'after the nukes'. Write up her entry for this same period, from her meeting with Danny to her statement 'We've got to be as hard as they are, Danny boy–or harder.'

AT THE end Danny is crying as he comes to the conclusion 'Hardness versus compassion. No contest.' This makes a powerful image. Write a poem using this image and/or any other images which you feel convey your own response to a possible nuclear tragedy.

Extended Study of Julius Lester

Julius Lester is one of the major American writers who has opened out black experience for young people. Many of his stories have a factual basis. After wider reading of his works, write your assessment of the contribution he has made to children's literature. You may wish to consider the following statements and find examples from his writing which support them.

JULIUS LESTER has enabled us to hear the voices of people without power and silenced by society.

HIS PORTRAYAL of white people from the perspective of his black characters is not flattering, but just.

HIS SHORT stories reveal human courage in the face of enormous odds. For example, Allen in *Basketball Game* reveals the courage of a young person who desperately wants to believe it is possible to move above the racism of white American society and have a normal relationship with Rebecca. At the end he is bitterly disappointed.

Why do you think Julius Lester created this ending and what is your personal response to it? Consider what comment he may be making about the overall structure of society–the way it is organised and the ways in which it directs the behaviour of most people.

CONSIDER THE short story 'Louis' (in *Long Journey Home*) where the young man Louis, who has escaped from slavery, has to separate his personal liking for his former 'master' from the white man's role as a slave-owner who has the power to sell him. If the white man had not been a slave-owner and Louis a slave, they might have been friends. Consider this in relation to *Basketball Game*. What is Julius Lester saying about racism? Is he showing it to be something deeper than just prejudiced feelings and opinions?

TWO OTHER major writers about black American experience are Mildred Taylor and Rosa Guy. If you have read some of their works, you could extend your study. How do you feel they complement the knowledge you have gained from reading Julius Lester?

APART FROM their literary importance, do you think these writers are politically important? Is it possible for someone writing about social issues to be non-political? Are these issues which you think people of your age should know about? (You can consider these last two questions in relation to Julius Lester alone if necessary.)

EXTENDED STUDY ON GENERATIONS

In many of these extracts, stories and poems there is a strong contrast in the responses of young people and adults. The adults often seem to accept the situation as it is, while the young people want to change it. Select a range of pieces in which to examine the relationship between the generations.

You might consider the following issues:

HOW DO you explain the attitudes of each of the adult characters who accept or put up with life as it is? Examine each in detail. (Does Eloy in 'Private Eloy' help you understand what may have happened to some of these older characters and the pressures to conform?) In what ways are their younger counterparts different? Do you think they may be able to remain resistent as they grow older, and if so, how? Consider the writers themselves.

CAN YOU find signs that some of the adults still experience conflict in themselves about accepting conditions which the younger generation try to reject?

THERE ARE examples of people who don't fit the pattern described, e.g. in 'Private Eloy', 'If Someone Were To Ask Me...', 'True Grit, Hard Graft'. In what way are the people here different? Look again, particularly at the poem 'Grandad' and consider what gives the final image its power.

DRAWING ON your own experiences, what are *your* observations about attitudes in different generations? If you think there is a general pattern, can you find evidence which does not fit this? How hopeful are you about change?

Extended Study on Racism

A theme running throughout this collection is that of experiences in childhood and adolescence which enable young people to learn about their society and some of the powerful forces within it.

Write an essay in which you focus on the pieces which reveal young people learning for themselves about racism. You might use the following ideas, amongst any others you wish to develop.

DESCRIBE THE particular experiences of each young character selected. Then consider whether there are any similarities in their responses.

LOOK AT the dates involved. The order in which items have been placed in this collection is broadly chronological. Find out about various struggles for equality, justice and Black rights. You could learn something about their development in the USA from *Black Lives White Worlds* by Keith Ajegbo and from the selection edited by Roxy Harris in *Being Black*. These ideas were of course not confined to the USA. After your research you could write about whether, and how, you think the pieces in this collection reflect the time in which they are set. (For instance, do you think the reggae hit 'Young, Gifted And Black'–which became number five in the British charts in 1970– would have made it to the charts in 1960?)

THERE IS a gap of almost sixty years between the South African experiences in *Tell Freedom* and those of 'Homecoming' and 'If Someone Were To Ask Me...'. Find out about the development of apartheid. What do these extracts tell you about the society? The imprisoned grandfather in the poem 'Grandad' would have been growing up in the same period as the boy Lee in *Tell Freedom*. Write about the connections which could be made between these two pieces. You would find it helpful to read some of the statements made in court by political prisoners in South Africa, in which they speak of some of the experiences which led them to take action against apartheid (in *The Sun Will Rise*, edited by Mary Benson).

WRITE ABOUT your personal response to racism and the material in this collection. Have any pieces had a particular impact on you and in what way?

EXTENDED STUDY ON YOUNG PEOPLE'S AWARENESS

The author of the poem 'The Child' is pessimistic. This is what he wrote about his poem when it appeared in *City Lines: Poems By London School Students* (ILEA English Centre, 1982):

> *The idea for the poem was sparked off while I was listening to a record. The lyrics immediately made me think of a child, by the sea, playing with sand on the beach. At the same time I remembered how I'd once been like that myself; yet now I'm so different. I could see that one day I'd be like all the adults around me. I'm gradually losing all my innocence all the time – and there's nothing I can do to prevent it.*
>
> *Unfortunately as we grow, we gain the capability to destroy – only a child with its total innocence lacks the ability to do this. But we were all like that once! When I was ten, I didn't want to get any older, but I was determined that I'd always understand the feelings of a child when I grew up. I've not even finished growing up yet, and already I cannot identify with a ten year old and deep down I know that ultimately I'll be like all the adults who sometimes don't understand me now. I'll lose contact as I get older and become something different.*
>
> *And ironically, it's only when you're older and you have lost your inno-cence that you can look back and see how wonderful it was to be unaware of what the future held, and you could play uninhibitedly, with no respon-sibilities. Be careful: that's The Child.*

DO YOU believe with David Upshall that 'There's but one restricted way for you to form'? Accabre Huntley was only ten when her poem 'Free As I Know' was first published in her own collection *At School Today* (Bogle-L'Ouverture, 1977). Yet she expresses calmly a very mature idea: 'I am free as I know'. It seems that she was already aware of more than just playing with sand on the beach. Do you think she will be as helpless to prevent her attitudes being changed– and her inner freedom being crushed–as the child in David Upshall's poem?

USING KNOWLEDGE you have gained from this collection and other sources, as well as your own experiences, write an essay on the development of social and political awareness in young people. You might consider:

– different levels and kinds of awareness that arise from various childhood experiences
– the pressures to conform to the way the society is presently organised
– the abilities to resist such pressures
– what importance you place on people of your age gaining political understanding
– what sort of issues you think students of your age should be

allowed to consider, and to what sort of material they should be given access.

Give examples of the effect certain reading has had on you in developing your own wider awareness. Where appropriate, use quotations to illustrate your points, and always provide reasons for your views.

EXTENDED STUDY ON AUTOBIOGRAPHY

This collection contains a number of pieces which are autobiographical. Some are extracts from full length books, others essays and poems. Read at least one full length autobiography as well (see the list of Further Reading), before writing an essay on this form of writing. You might consider the following:

AUTOBIOGRAPHY ALLOWS the writer to communicate experiences which have been important for her or his own development and to reflect aloud. Quote a variety of examples.

WHAT IS your own response in each case to the examples you have quoted. What is the effect of the author's direct tone? Have you ever been put off by an author's tone?

HOW IMPORTANT to you is the vividness of the author's descriptions? Give examples.

WHY DO you think a writer might choose to deal with personal experiences in a novel, rather than write an autobiography?

LOOK FOR examples of fictional writing where the author uses the first person. Examine the effect. Try rewriting certain passages of first person writing into third, and vice versa, to see what happens. Discuss the use of first and third person narrative in your essay using quotations to illustrate your points.

Further Reading

Note Where there is a range in the reading levels of books, the easiest to read have been listed first.

Tell Freedom *by Peter Abrahams (Faber & Faber, 1981), 'Homecoming' by Lerato Nomvuyo Mzamane, and 'If Someone Were To Ask Me...' by Manelisi all derive from South Africa. 'Homecoming' was specially written for this collection and 'If Someone Were To Ask Me...' is also previously unpublished. There is a wealth of other literature, including the following works.*

FICTION

Journey To Jo'burg: A South African Story, Beverley Naidoo, Longman Knock-outs (1985); Other Award winner 1985

Waiting For The Rain, Sheila Gordon, Orchard Books (1987) – novel

The Soweto I Love, Sipho Sepamla, Rex Collings (1977)–poems

Debbie Go Home, Alan Paton, Penguin (1965)–short stories

A Dry White Season, Andre Brink, Flamingo (1979)–novel

Hungry Flames And Other Black South African Short Stories, ed. Mbulelo Mzamane, Longman African Classics (1986)

Call Me Not A Man, Mtutuzeli Matshoba, Longman Drumbeat (1981)–short stories

The Children Of Soweto: A Trilogy, Mbulelo Mzamane, Longman Drumbeat (1982)

My Cousin Comes To Jo'burg, Mbulelo Mzamane, Longman Drumbeat (1980)

Selected Stories, Nadine Gordimer, Penguin (1983)

Six Feet Of The Country, Nadine Gordimer, Penguin (1982)–short stories

Wild Conquest, Peter Abrahams, Penguin (1966)–historical novel

Cross Of Gold, Lauretta Ngcobo, Longman Drumbeat (1981) – novel

'Master Harold'... And The Boys, Athol Fugard, OUP (1983)–play

Statements, three plays devised by Athol Fugard, John Kani and Winston Ntshona: 'Siswe Bansi Is Dead'; 'The Island'; 'Statements After The Arrest Under The Immorality Act', OUP (1974)

Poets To The People, ed. by Barry Feinberg, Heinemann (1980) – poetry

NON-FICTION

The Child Is Not Dead – Youth Resistance In South Africa, compiled by Ann Harries, Roger Diski, Alasdair Brown, BDAF*/ ILEA Learning Resources Branch (1986), Martin Luther King Memorial Prize

South Africa The Cordoned Heart: Essays By Twenty South African Photographers, ed. Omar Badsha, W.W. Norton (1986)

We Make Freedom: Women In South Africa, Beata Lipman, Pandora, (1984)–interviews

Kaffir Boy: Growing Out Of Apartheid, Mark Mathabane, Pan (1987)–

autobiography

The Sun Will Rise – Statements From The Dock By Southern African Political Prisoners, ed. by Mary Benson, IDAF (1981)

Island In Chains: Ten Years On Robben Island By Prisoner 885/63, as told by Indres Naidoo to Albie Sachs, Penguin (1982)–autobiography

Part Of My Soul, Winnie Mandela ed. by Anne Benjamin, Penguin (1985)–autobiography

Censoring Reality: An Examination Of Non-Fiction Books On South Africa, Beverley Naidoo, ILEA Centre for Anti-racist Education/BDAF* (1985)

The Apartheid Handbook: A Guide To South Africa's Everyday Racial Policies, Roger Omond, Penguin (1985)

* The British Defence and Aid Fund for Southern Africa also publishes a list of resource materials for schools. Address on p157.

*   *   *

Basketball Game *by Julius Lester, Penguin (1972) and* I Know Why The Caged Bird Sings *by Maya Angelou, Virago (1984), both derive from the USA. Highly recommended background reading is the collection of writings compiled by Keith Ajegbo in* Black Lives White Worlds, *Cambridge Educational (1982), Other Award winner 1982. A few of many other titles are:*

Long Journey Home: Stories from Black History, Julius Lester, Longman Knockouts (1978)

To Be A Slave, Julius Lester, Puffin (1973)–documentary

A Taste Of Freedom, Julius Lester, Longman Knockouts (1973)–stories

Roll Of Thunder, Hear My Cry, Mildred Taylor, Puffin (1980)–novel

Let The Circle Be Unbroken, Mildred Taylor, Puffin (1984)–novel

The Friends, Rosa Guy, Puffin (1977)–novel

Edith Jackson, Rosa Guy, Puffin (1985)–novel

The Disappearance, Rosa Guy, Puffin (1985)–novel

Stamping, Shouting And Singing Home, Lisa Evans (1985)–play. Photocopy available at cost from The SCYPT Library, Standing Conference of Young People's Theatre, Dept. of Humanities, University of Kent and Canterbury, Canterbury, Kent.

And Still I Rise, Maya Angelou, Virago (1986)–poetry

Green Days By The River, Michael Anthony, Heinemann (1973)–novel

Black Boy, Richard Wright, Longman (1970)–autobiography

Being Black: Selections From Soledad Brother And Soul On Ice, ed. Roxy Harris, New Beacon Books (1981)–autobiography

Brown Girl, Brownstones, Paule Marshall, Virago (1982)–novel

Betsey Brown, Ntozake Shange, Methuen (1985)–novel

Go Tell It On The Mountain, James Baldwin, Corgi (1984)–novel

The Fire Next Time, James Baldwin, Penguin (1970)–letters

The Autobiography Of Malcolm X as told to Alex Haley, Penguin (1970)

'Private Eloy' by Samuel Feijoo comes from Cuba: An Anthology For Young People, *Young World Books (1983).*

Friedrich, Hans Peter Richter, Heinemann (1978)–novel

I Was There, Hans Peter Richter, Kestrel Books (1973)–novel

Time Of The Young Soldiers, Hans Peter Richter, Kestrel (1976)–novel

(Note: *I Was There and Time Of The Young Soldiers* form a trilogy with *Friedrich* and only take on their full meaning after reading the latter, set during the early years of the Nazis' rise to power)

The Wave: The Classroom Experiment That Went Too Far, Morton Rhue, Puffin, (1982)–novel

The Deserter, Nigel Gray, Harper & Row (1979)–novel

Sixty-Five, V.S. Reid, Longman (1980)–historical novel

Talking In Whispers, James Watson, Fontana (1985)–novel; Other Award winner 1983

Let's Visit Cuba, John Griffiths, Burke (1983)–non-fiction

Castro, Paul Humphrey, Wayland (1981) – non-fiction

Caribbean In The Twentieth Century, John Griffiths, Batsford (1984)–non-fiction

Weep Not, Child, James Ngugi, Heinemann African Writers Series (1964)–novel

Writing In Cuba Since The Revolution, ed. Andrew Salkey, Bogle-L'Ouverture (1977)–fiction and non-fiction prose, poetry

*　　　　*　　　　*

Hand On The Sun *by Tariq Mehmood, Penguin (1983) and the essay 'Young Gifted And Black', written for this collection by Beverley Naidoo, are both set in England.*

Home Front, Derek Bishton & John Reardon, Jonathan Cape (1984)–photographic essay

Easter Monday Blues, Accabre Huntley, Bogle-L'Ouverture (1983)–poetry

Livingroom (especially 'A Spade Is A Spade' by Joyce Alexander), Black Ink Collective (1983)–young writers' collection

Our Lives: Young People's Autobiographies, ed. Paul Ashton et al, ILEA English Centre (1979)

Come To Mecca And Other Stories, Farrukh Dhondy, Fontana (1978); Other Award winner 1979

East End At Your Feet, Farrukh Dhondy, Macmillan Topliner (1976)–short stories; Other Award winner 1977

So This Is England: A Prose Anthology, Peckham Publishing Project (1984)

Motherland: West Indian Women To Britain In The 1950s, Elyse Dodgson, Heinemann (1984)–interviews and play; Other Award winner 1985

Further Reading

The School Leaver, Michael McMillan, Black Ink Publications (1978)–play

News For Babylon: The Chatto Book Of West Indian-British Poetry, ed. James Berry, Chatto & Windus (1984)

Dread Beat And Blood, Linton Kwesi Johnson, Bogle-L'Ouverture (1975)–poetry

The Lonely Londoners, Samuel Selvon, Longman Drumbeat (1979)–novel

Absolute Beginners, Colin MacInnes, Allison & Busby (1980)–novel

City Of Spades, Colin MacInnes, Allison & Busby (1980)–novel

*   *   *

'India' by Ravinder Randhawa first appeared in the collection More To Life Than Mr Right: Stories For Young Feminists, *compiled by Rosemary Stones, Piccadilly Press (1985), Fontana (1987).*

Sumitra's Story, Rukshana Smith, Bodley Head (1982)–novel

Parveen, Anna Mehdevi, Chatto & Windus (1975)–novel

It's My Life, Robert Leeson, Fontana (1980)–novel

Ruby, Rosa Guy, Gollancz (1981)–novel

Girls Are Powerful: Young Women's Writing From Spare Rib, ed. Susan Hemmings, Sheba (1982)

True To Life: Writings By Young Women, ed. Susan Hemmings, Sheba (1986)

Wasted Women Friends And Lovers, Black Ink Collective (1980)–plays, poetry, prose

Finding A Voice: Asian Women In Britain, Amrit Wilson, Virago (1978)–non-fiction prose

Selling Pictures, teaching pack, British Film Institute (1983)

Gregory's Girl, Andrew Bethell, 'Act Now' series, Cambridge University Press (1983)–play

Watchers And Seekers: Creative Writing By Black Women In Britain, ed. Rhonda Cobham & Merle Collins, The Women's Press (1987)–prose and poetry

Second-Class Citizen, Buchi Emecheta, Fontana (1974)–novel

A Wicked Old Woman, Ravinder Randhawa, The Women's Press (1987) – novel

The Woman Warrior: Memoirs of a Girlhood among Ghosts, Maxine Hong Kingston, Picador (1981)–novel

Portraits, Kate Chopin, The Women's Press (1979)–short stories

The Charlotte Perkins Gilman Reader, Charlotte Perkins Gilman, The Women's Press (1981)–short stories

*   *   *

'*Small Avalanches*' *by Joyce Carol Oates comes from* The Secret Self: Short Stories By Women, *ed. Hermione Lee, Dent & Sons (1985). Apart from this collection, readers will also find connections in* Girls Are Powerful *and* True To Life, *listed above, as well as in:*

'Are You Difficult' in *Black Ink No. 1*, Black Ink Collective (1978)–short story

'Crazy Mary' by Claude McKay in *Best West Indian Short Stories*, ed. Kenneth Ramchand, Nelson Caribbean (1982)

Yesterday Today Tomorrow, ed. Jane Leggett and Ros Moger, The English Centre (1986)–poetry

I Know Why The Caged Bird Sings, Maya Angelou, Virago (1984)–autobiography

Cry Hard And Swim, Jacqueline Spring, Virago (1987)

*   *   *

'*True Grit, Hard Graft*' *by Dawn Newton first appeared under the title* '*Why Did We Fall Apart and How Did We Come Back Together?*' *in the anthology* More Valuable Than Gold: A Collection of Writings On The Miners' Strike Of 1984–1985 By Striking Miners' Children, *ed. Martin Hoyles and Susan Hemmings, Martin Hoyles (1985). It is available (£2 incl. p&p) from MVTG, 10 West Bank, London N16 5DG. Dawn Newton was fifteen when she wrote the piece.*

Twopence A Tub, Susan Price, Faber (1975)–novel; Other Award winner 1975

The Nature Of The Beast, Janni Howker, Fontana (1986)–novel

A Sound Of Chariots, Mollie Hunter, Hamish Hamilton (1972)–novel

Johnny Jarvis, Nigel Williams, Puffin Plus (1983)–novel

Dockie, Martin Ballard, Fontana (1974)–novel

Will Of Iron, Gerard Melia, Longman Knockouts (1983)–play; Other Award winner 1983

Spring Offensive, Ray Speakman and Dereck Nicholls, 'Act Now' series. Cambridge University Press (1982)–play

City Lines: Poems By London School Students, ILEA English Centre (1983)

Stepney Words, children's poetry compiled by Chris Searle and Ron McCormick, Centreprise (1973)

*   *   *

Brother In The Land by Robert Swindells, Puffin (1985) was an Other Award winner in 1984. Readers are strongly recommended to read the full novel as well as:

The Hiroshima Story, Toshi Maruki, A&C Black (1983)–illustrated witness account.

Sadako And The Thousand Paper Cranes, Eleanor Coerr, Hodder and Stoughton (1982)–biography

When The Wind Blows, Raymond Briggs, Penguin (1982)– illustrated story; Other Award winner 1982

Z for Zachariah, Robert O'Brien, Fontana (1976)–novel
The Burning Book, Maggie Gee, Faber (1983)–novel
Hiroshima, John Hershey, Penguin (1986)–non-fiction
The Nuclear War Game, Adam Suddaby, Longman (1983)–non-fiction
The Crucible Of Despair: The Effects of Nuclear War, Anthony Tucker & John
Gleisner, Menard (1982)–non-fiction

ADDRESSES FOR COMMUNITY PUBLICATIONS

Black Ink Collective, 258 Coldharbour Lane, London SW9
Bogle L'Ouverture Publications, 5a Chignell Place, London W13
British Defence and Aid Fund for Southern Africa (BDAFSA), Canon Collins
    House, 64 Essex Road, London N1 8LR
British Film Institute, Dean Street, London W1
Centreprise, 136 Kingsland High Street, London E8
ILEA English Centre Publications, available through NATE, 49
    Broomgrove Road, Sheffield S10 2NA
ILEA Learning Resources Centre, 275 Kennington Lane, London SE11 5QZ
Peckham Publishing Project, The Bookplace, 13 Peckham High Street,
    London SE15 5EB
New Beacon Books, 76 Stroud Green Road, London N4 3EN
Young World Books, c/o Liberation, 490 Kingsland Road, London E8

Acknowledgements

The editor and publishers would like to express thanks to the following for permission to reproduce stories, extracts and poems in this anthology:

Faber and Faber Limited for the extract from *Tell Freedom* by Peter Abrahams.

Virago Press Limited for the edited extract from *I Know Why The Caged Bird Sings* and poem 'Still I Rise' by Maya Angelou.

Penguin Books Limited for the edited extract from *Basketball Game* by Julius Lester (Kestrel Books, 1974) and for the extract from *Hand On The Sun* by Tariq Mehmood (Penguin Books, 1983).

Indiana University Press for 'Once Upon A Time' by Gabriel Okara from *Poems From Black Africa* edited by Langston Hughes.

Young World Books for 'Private Eloy' by Samuel Feijoo from *Cuba: An Anthology For Young People*.

Joyce Carol Oates for 'Small Avalanches' from *The Goddess And Other Women* published by Victor Gollancz.

Allison & Busby, a division of W. H. Allen Publishers, for 'Back In The Playground Blues' by Adrian Mitchell.

Beverley Naidoo for her personal essay written especially for this anthology 'Young, Gifted and Black'.

Piccadilly Press Limited for 'India' by Ravinder Randhawa from *More To Life Than Mr Right* edited by Rosemary Stones.

Sheba Feminist Press for 'A Tanned Version' and 'Looking' by Hummarah Quddoos from *True To Life: Writings By Young*

Women edited by Susan Hemmings.

Dawn Newton for 'True Grit, Hard Graft' from *More Valuable Than Gold: A Collection Of Writings On The Miners' Strike Of 1984–85 By Striking Miners' Children* edited by Martin Hoyles and Susan Hemmings.

Lerato Nomvuyo Mzamane for 'Homecoming'.

Manelisi for 'If Someone Were To Ask Me...'.

Oxford University Press for the extracts from *Brother In The Land* by Robert Swindells (1984).

The ILEA English Centre for 'The Child' by David Upshall from *City Lines*.

Bogle–L'Ouverture Publications Limited for 'Free As I Know' by Accabre Huntley from *At School Today*.

Whilst every effort has been made to contact the copyright-holders, this has not proved to be possible in every case.